Hope Valley

Also by John Manuel

The Natural Traveler Along North Carolina's Coast

The Canoeist: A Memoir

For Cathy

ISBN 978-0-9981112-0-9 (paperback)
ISBN 978-0-9981112-1-6 (electronic book)

Cover art by Dick Hill, Hill Studio
dickhillstudio.com

Book design by the Frogtown Bookmaker
frogtownbookmaker.com

Published by Red Lodge Press,
redlodgepress.com

Hope Valley

A Novel

John Manuel

Red Lodge Press
Durham, North Carolina

Chapter 1

Hurley Cates stood in the crumbling civic center parking lot waiting for the preacher to give him a sign. Reverend Shively reached into the back of the church van and pulled out a placard—*The Wages of Sin is Death.*

"This one's for you, Hurley."

He took it with a grim nod and let it hang in the space between him and Opal. He was not a sign-carrying type. Never been in a situation where he felt he had to pass judgment on others. But this was different. His hometown of Durham was being invaded by gays and lesbians and, like slugs crossing the patio, they needed to be stamped out.

"Opal, can I get you one?" the Reverend said to Hurley's wife. He pulled out the next sign—*Fornicators!*

She shook her head. "I'll let Hurley do the carrying."

"Go on out to the street, then. You'll see the others."

Opal clutched his arm as they headed for the alley. They'd been married fifty years, but he could count on one hand the number of times she'd held onto him like this. Was she afraid of the marchers, or was it something else?

Out on Main Street, he spotted a dozen other members of the church standing by the curb. He took comfort in their number, steered Opal beside Tom and Ellie Murphy.

"I see you wore your mowing outfit," Tom said.

Hurley glanced down at his brown khaki work pants and shirt. "What's wrong with that?"

Opal smiled. "He'd wear that outfit to church if I didn't make him change."

Ellie wrapped her arms around her shoulders. "I should've worn my wool coat. It's cold as the dickens for May."

"Sun'll be over those buildings soon," Tom said. "You'll be alright."

Hurley peered at the empty facades along Main Street, like so many rotten teeth. The time was these sidewalks were full of people. Since the tobacco and textile mills had closed, it had been all downhill. Maybe that's why the lesbians had picked Durham to move to. They thought nobody would notice.

"When's the last time you were downtown, Tom?" he said.

"Probably three years ago. '82. Had to pull jury duty."

Ellie pointed across the street at the marbled facade of the Belk-Leggett's Department Store. "Good old Belk's. I used to get my dress shoes over there. Third floor."

"I got all my school clothes there," Opal said. "It was a nice store."

"Everything's out at the mall, now," Ellie said.

He studied the crowd gathering across the street—young women wearing silk scarves and knit caps, men with short beards and tight-fitting pants. Were they all homos and lesbians? They seemed to be in high spirits.

He nudged Tom. "What's your sign say?"

"Abomination."

"Mine's *Wages of Sin is Death*. Are we supposed to hold 'em up the whole time?"

Tom shook his head. "I'm waiting 'til the sissies come by."

Reverend Shively came out from the alley clutching a megaphone. He fumbled with the trigger; the megaphone screeched.

"TESTING. TESTING."

Shively was new to Mount Moriah Baptist. Hurley had yet to decide whether he liked him or not. The Reverend was from the mountains, a fire and brimstone preacher where the others had been soft-spoken types. He'd woken the congregation up, that was for sure. When someone says you're likely to go to hell, you pay attention.

Down the street, snare drums snapped up a marching beat. A bass drum kicked in. Opal furrowed her brow. "Sounds like a school band."

Here they came, led by a major in a plumed hat and leather chaps.

"Where did they get those uniforms?" Ellie said.

Tom sniffed. "Stole 'em, probably."

The major blew his whistle and the horn section struck up *When the Saints Come Marching In.*

"Get your signs up," the Reverend said.

He opened a Bible and read into the megaphone as the marching band approached. "We are in the midst of lions. I lie among ravenous beasts, men whose teeth are spears..."

Hurley held up his sign. The young people across the street hooted. "We love you, man."

What were they talking about?

Behind the marching band, male and female couples dressed in black leather walked hand in hand. Two of the women stopped to kiss. He shook his sign. Ellie shouted, "Boo!"

Down the street, a powder blue Chrysler convertible neared, windshield glinting in the morning sun. A blond-haired man with impossibly white teeth smiled and waved from atop the back seat. Mayor MacAfee. Everything about the man turned his stomach. He was young, good-looking, a Duke grad and a Democrat.

"Did you hear about the recall petition?" Tom said. "People want MacAfee voted out for endorsing the parade."

"I'll go for that," he said.

McAfee smiled and waved. Nothing fazed him.

A line of floats followed, identified by colorful signs—the Durham Gay-Lesbian Alliance, The Independent newspaper, Planned Parenthood.

"There's the abortion people," Opal said.

Two women seated on the float tossed small packets to the crowd. One of the packets skittered to Opal's feet. She picked up the condom, stared at it, and dropped it with a look of horror.

Tom winked at him. "She thought it was candy."

A squad of motorcycles approached, the riders staring through mirrored sunglasses. He read the slogan on the back of their black leather jackets. "*Dykes on Bikes*."

He nudged Opal. "They's women!"

A group of marchers followed, wearing lady's underwear over blue jeans, gaudy wigs, and high heels. They blew whistles and air horns.

"Which are these?" Ellie asked.

Opal shook her head. "I'm all confused."

With the passing of the last group, the noise subsided. This looked to be the end of the parade, just some hangers on walking along behind. He lowered his sign, took a pouch of Red Man out of his coat pocket and shoved a chaw between his cheek and gum.

The people kept coming, more and more breaking away from the curb and joining in a silent march. These were ordinary looking people—older couples, parents with children. Why in the world would they join in if they weren't gay or lesbian?

Tom nudged him. "Look what I got." From his coat pocket, Tom produced an egg. "Let's see how good my aim is."

At the very end of the parade, a pretty dark-haired girl walked hand-in-hand with a heavy-set person in short hair and faded jean jacket. Hurley was trying to figure out if this was a man or a woman when Tom threw his egg and hit the person in the back of the head. Bystanders erupted in laughter. The woman—that's what she was—cringed as the yolk slid down the back of her head. She turned to clear the mess with her bare hand and, for a moment, he thought he was looking at his daughter, Patsy.

Tom shouted, "Go back to New York!"

Hurley lowered his sign, the anguish in the woman's face rendering him suddenly weak. Opal, too, looked upset.

He took her by the elbow. "Let's go on home."

Chapter 2

Hurley put on his khaki pants and shirt, stood before the spotted mirror, and felt the stubble on his lantern jaw. He could go another day without a shave. He licked his hand and smoothed his thinning gray hair.

The floorboards creaked as he followed the hallway into the kitchen. Opal stood before the sink, her white hair backlit like a frosted globe. She was looking kind of stooped these days, something he thought to mention, but decided it was better left alone.

"Coffee's ready," Opal said. "I'll have the biscuits by the time you get the paper."

He stared out the window at his son's brick ranch house on the right hand side of the drive. "Buddy up yet?"

"I haven't seen him."

"He needs to mow that lawn."

"You've said that twice already."

He took a toothpick from the container and set it in the corner of his mouth. He put on his ballcap and headed out the front door.

Standing on the porch, he scanned his five-acre lawn where it sloped down to Hope Valley Road. He'd done a good job mowing, no stray blades around the big oak trees. Buddy's lawn was another matter. Across the shared driveway, the grass stuck up a good six inches, weeds even higher. People passing by must think he and Opal had raised a worthless son.

He stepped off the porch and headed down for the paper. Spring was coming on, new leaves in the woods glowing like colored glass. A bluebird dropped from a low branch and landed on the lawn beside him. Funny little things. They'd follow right behind him in the riding mower picking up the injured bugs. This one must imagine the sound of his footsteps would scare a grub out of its hole.

At the bottom of the drive, he picked up the paper and glanced at the headline—*Gay Parade Deemed A Success*. What a load of crap. For the third time this year, he promised himself he'd cancel his subscription.

Across the road, one of Marvin's cows started to bawl. A second chimed in, then a third. They were all lined up at the fence looking toward the house. Something not right about that. He checked both ways and headed across the road.

Marvin's one-story farmhouse stood in the low ground, half hidden behind overgrown privet bushes. The rich smell of cow manure drifted from the pasture as he walked down the gravel drive. Unbroken walnuts rolled underfoot. It'd been awhile since Marvin had driven his car.

He stepped onto the porch and knocked on the door. He knocked again. "Marvin, it's me."

The door cracked open to reveal a gaunt face and hollow eyes.

"Your cows are raising a ruckus," Hurley said. "Ain't you fed 'em yet?"

Marvin stared past him. "I kindly forgot."

Hurley stepped into the living room. "Feels cold in here. You got your heat on?" He went to the thermostat. It was turned up to seventy.

"You must have let your propane run out," he said. "You need to call the man and get him to refill it."

"I've got the woodstove."

"You need to use it."

He stared around the room. Newspapers and disassembled tools covered the floor. An open tin of cat food sat on the coffee table. Beside Marvin's stuffed chair lay a double-barrel shotgun. He picked it up and presented it to Marvin. "What do you have this out for?"

Marvin mumbled something about burglars.

"There ain't no burglars around here," Hurley said. He broke open the chamber. "One shell?"

Marvin slumped into his stuffed chair, his eyes gone vacant. "I ain't no good no more."

Hurley put the gun down and cleared a space on the couch. "What do you mean no good?"

The old man waved at the window. "There's no money in them cows. I might as well turn 'em loose."

"You were never in it for the money."

He looked around the room. "This place is a mess. When's the last time you had anyone to visit?"

"I don't get any visitors."

"What about your sister?"

"I haven't seen her in a year."

"Maybe you ought to think about selling, move into a retirement home."

Marvin sniffed. "Who's gonna buy this place, interest rates at 13 percent? I'm not one for retirement anyway. Can't play cards."

Outside, the cows resumed their bellowing. "You want me to help you with the feeding?"

"I can do it."

"I know you can. Are you?"

"Soon as you leave."

Hurley was not convinced. He might have turned Marvin from the headlights, but there was no telling if he'd stay out of the road.

He took the shell out of the chamber, and slid it in his pocket. "I'll be checking on you, now. You need me, call me."

* * *

Opal looked up as he came through the door. "I put your breakfast back in the oven," she said. "What took you so long?"

He hung his ballcap on the hook and set the newspaper on the table. "Marvin's cows were raising a ruckus. I went to look in on him."

"Is something wrong?"

"He had his shotgun out. I think he was ready to use it on himself."

"Oh, Lord." Opal wiped her hands on the dish towel. "Maybe we should get Reverend Shively to pay him a visit."

He scoffed. "Marvin ain't been to church in years. Besides, what's the preacher going to say? Farming's done in this county. What you make from cattle or corn won't begin to cover your taxes."

"He needs to sell that farm and go into retirement."

"What I told him. He don't want to go."

She opened the refrigerator and rummaged through the contents. "I've got this ham and beans from yesterday. Why don't you take him that?"

"He's got plenty of food."

"Now, you've got me worried." She took the plate of bacon and eggs out of the oven and set it on the kitchen table. "That man spends too much time alone."

"He'll be alright."

She poured him a cup of coffee. "Leanne called while you were out. She invited us over for pie."

"Pie?"

"I know, it doesn't sound right. I hope she and Buddy aren't splitting up."

* * *

As he and Opal approached the brick rancher, a yellow mutt came out from under his bush. He touched his nose to Hurley's pants.

"Git!"

Opal frowned. "You don't need to take it out on poor Gus."

She knocked on the side door.

"Perfect timing," Leanne said. "I just got the ice cream out of the freezer."

Hurley hated that phony smile, the green eyes and the sprayed helmet of hair. She ought to hang a sign around her neck *Do Not Touch*.

The shag carpet in the family room had just been vacuumed. The aroma of pecan pie filled the air. Something was definitely up.

They settled into the couch.

"Buddy, your parents are here."

Down the hall came his son dressed in brown pants and a yellow cowboy shirt, holding his Bible like a favorite doll. Buddy had inherited most of Hurley's physical traits—long legs, big ears, lantern jaw—but his head had gotten stretched out during childbirth. Riley, Hurley's fishing friend, joked that Buddy looked like a reflection of his father in a funhouse mirror.

"Pa." Buddy offered a limp handshake and sat at the dinner table, his hand resting on the Good Book. Hurley didn't mind that his son was religious, but it bothered him that he relied on scripture for things that were a matter of common sense. The boy could spend an hour searching through those pages to figure out if it was a good idea to get a haircut.

"How's work?" Hurley said.

"O.K. City's going to hire me to help put in a sewer line over in Monkey Top. Should be some time next month."

"What about that Research Park? I hear there's high-paying work over there."

"That's out of my territory."

Leanne cut the pie and dished it onto plates.

"Ice cream for you, Hurley? I know Opal wants it."

He nodded.

"This was made with pecans from your tree," Leanne said. "They were lying in the driveway, so I figured you wouldn't mind."

"I shot four squirrels out of that tree last fall," he said.

Leanne handed him a plate. "Yes, we heard. Seven o'clock on a Sunday morning."

She cut herself a piece and sat next to Buddy. Whatever he had to say was making him nervous.

"What's going on?" Hurley said.

Buddy pulled on his earlobe. "We're kindly thinking of selling the house."

Opal dropped her fork. Hurley frowned. "What'choo talkin' about?"

Buddy glanced at Leanne. "We'd like to be a little more on our own."

"On your own?"

"Somewhere further away."

"What's wrong with where you're at?"

Leanne smiled. "I think you know."

He struggled to keep himself in his chair. He'd strangle that woman right now if Opal weren't in the room.

"When are you thinking of moving?" Opal said.

"As soon as we can sell the house," Buddy said. "We've made an offer on a place off of Sparger Road."

"Isn't that's on the other side of town?"

Hurley figured this had to be Leanne's doing. Buddy would never have the guts.

"So that's how you do me?" he said to Buddy. "I give you the land and you turn around and sell it?"

"Pa, that was twenty years ago."

He glared at his son, waiting for him to surrender, but Leanne kept her hand clamped on his. He tried softening his tone. "You want to let your grass grow, I won't bother you about it," he said.

Leanne burst out laughing. "You're a day late and a dollar short on that one."

The blood rushed to his face. He put down his pie and stood. "Come on, Opal. We've got things to do."

When Opal hesitated, he lifted her by the arm off the couch.

Buddy jumped up and followed them to the door. "We'll be over for Sunday dinner."

"The hell you say."

Chapter 3

Outside in the drive, Opal stood in stunned silence. If Buddy left, who knew what kind of people would move in and what they might do with the property? All of Hurley's plans for keeping the hill the way he liked it could go up in smoke.

She stared down the hill where Marvin's cows grazed in the meadow. It was Marvin who'd sold them this land. She and Hurley were living with him after they were married, renting the extra bedroom in the farmhouse. They raised both of the children in that house, Patsy until she was six and Buddy four. By that time, they needed a larger place.

The hill was covered in trees then, with a cleared tobacco field in the back. Marvin offered to sell them all twenty acres after he'd had it timbered. Hurley asked if they could first mark a few trees to save for around their house site and he agreed.

On a sunny winter day, she, Hurley, and the two children headed across the road to find and mark the trees. Hope Valley was still dirt, the main route into Durham from out in the county, but rarely used on a Saturday morning. They crossed holding hands and scrambled up the red clay embankment.

Dry leaves crunched underfoot as they headed into the woods. Here and there, dark green ferns colored the forest floor. Hurley found a small cedar whose bark had been rubbed off by a buck. He explained to Patsy that the deer liked a springy tree to scrape the felt off their antlers.

"Why do they scrape the felt off?" she said.

"They want them horns to look nice and shiny for pretty girls like you."

Patsy laughed and ran on ahead. Buddy, meanwhile, clung to Opal's hand, slipping and falling on the leaves.

"Wait for Bud," she said. "He doesn't have your long legs."

Hurley slowed his pace as he reached the top of the hill. "Around here is where I was thinking."

At first, all Opal could see was trees, but the contours of the land soon became clear. She pictured the house with a porch looking out over the valley.

"We put in a lawn down to the road, we'll have a real good view," he said.

"That's an awful lot of grass."

He gave her his little smile, the one that politely said, "You don't know much, do you?"

Patsy found a shade tree that she liked, a big oak that split into two trunks just above the ground. Hurley shook his head. "That's a fork-ed tree, Patsy. It's like to break when it gets older."

"I like it," she said. "It's different."

Hurley studied the crotch for signs of rot. "O.K. If you want. I'll hang a tire swing from that branch."

He gave her an orange ribbon to mark the tree for the loggers. Buddy whined, "I wanna tie some trees."

"You ain't big enough to tie anything yet," Hurley said. "Look at your shoelaces flopping loose."

Opal retied Buddy's laces. "He wants to be part of this," she said. "Let him pick something."

Hurley gave his son a ribbon, which he proceeded to drape over a sapling. Opal spotted a dogwood, the spare branches reaching for patches of sunlight.

"This'll be pretty in the spring," she said. "I can see it outside the kitchen window."

She felt such joy, studying the trees this way. It was just like Hurley to think about what was worth saving, to imagine how it would look years from now, not to cut it all down and have to start from scratch.

* * *

The spring after Marvin timbered the hill, they were ready to start building. She and Hurley both worked downtown at American Tobacco during the day, so they had to hire out the construction. Merv Coleman and a couple of colored boys laid the foundation. Dale Addison and his son, Troy, did the carpentry. The house was shaped like an L with the long front facing the slope to catch the breeze and the kitchen in the back where it could shed the heat.

She didn't have much to say about the construction, but when it came to finishes, she let her preferences be known. She wanted linoleum floors in the kitchen, speckled to hide any spills. In the living room, she wanted heartpine floors and sage green wallpaper in a pattern featuring Revolutionary War soldiers standing at attention.

She furnished the house with her grandmother's Danny Thomas clock, sofa, and stuffed chair. She bought a Hoosier cabinet and a porcelain-top kitchen table with matching red and white chairs. Most important, she got a Maytag wringer washer on wheels that she could roll from the mudroom into the kitchen.

During the weekends while the contractors were working on the house, Hurley constructed the outbuildings—a barn, tool shed, chicken coop, and three-bay car shed at the top of the drive. He dragged flat stones out of the woods to use as corner posts and scrap lumber for the framing. Patsy helped measure and mark the boards, while Buddy brought handfuls of nails, half of which he dropped. The finished sheds stood in a neat line behind the house, their tin roofs shining in the sun. Hurley ran a tractor path in front of them and added a barn at the end.

Last of all came the landscaping. To complement the forked oak at the front of the house and the dogwood in back, Hurley planted pecan trees to either side. Everything else from the house down to the road he stumped, tilled and seeded in fescue—five acres of lawn for him to weed, mow, and worry over.

It took years for the lawn to come in thick, but Opal had to admit it was a handsome thing. From the front porch, you could see across to Marvin's house and the ridge beyond. You could watch the cars pass on Hope Valley Road, long enough to give those you knew a wave and for them to wave back. And you could see who was coming up the drive, most times for the better, some times for worse.

Chapter 4

Hurley was sitting on the front porch when his grandson's blue Firebird turned up the drive. Dwayne popped the clutch, sending a bucketful of gravel onto the lawn. He rumbled past the front porch and flashed Hurley a shit-eating grin.

Dwayne's wife, Dawn, got out of the passenger side and went in the back door, while the great grandchildren, Ricky and Little Dwayne, ran for the tire swing hanging from the forked oak.

"Gapaw, will you push us?" Ricky said.

Hurley shook his head. "I ain't pushing today."

Opal had insisted that they have family for Sunday dinner, despite what had happened with Buddy and Leanne earlier in the week. That didn't mean he had to be polite.

Dwayne ambled over with his hands in his pockets. His wild blue eyes and tobacco-stained teeth could scare a man, but Hurley wasn't impressed.

"How many times I tell you about popping that clutch?" he said.

Dwayne climbed the steps and stretched out on the swingseat. "You need to pave that drive. I can't get traction going up that hill."

"I don't need to do nothing because you say so."

Ricky sat in the tire swing and ordered his brother to push him. Little Dwayne was only half Ricky's size, blond-haired to his black, but he was strong as a bulldog. L. Dog they called him. He set the tire in motion, the rope creaking from the low branch of the forked oak.

The boys traded places, but instead of pushing, Ricky spun the tire around, trying to make his brother fall off.

Hurley scowled. "Boy, you quit that!"

L. Dog slid to the ground. "I'm gonna be sick."

Dwayne pointed to the newly-posted Century 21 sign down by the road. "What do you think of Daddy selling the house?"

Hurley spat.

"Pretty wild if you ask me," Dwayne said. "The thought of some stranger sleeping in my old bedroom. What if it's some fat old man with hair all over his back?"

Dawn came out on the porch. She kissed Hurley on the forehead and settled into the chair beside him. She was wearing her big hairdo piled on top of her head. He supposed that was the style for secretaries at IBM.

"You staying busy?" he asked.

"Very. We're putting in a new assembly line to make that PC Junior."

"That a computer?"

Dawn nodded. "They say in ten years, one in every five households will have one."

He sniffed. "Pencil works fine for me."

The door opened across the drive. Leanne and Buddy emerged from the ranch house, she with her casserole and he clutching his Bible.

"Did you hear Daddy had a little mishap at work?" Dwayne said. "He was digging a sewer line by that colored graveyard on Mangum Street. Hit one of the coffins and a bunch of black goo flowed out. A colored woman saw it, got all upset and called the city."

"They fire him?"

"If it was white, they would have. Imagine if it was one of your own in that coffin. 'Momma! Momma!' "

Dawn frowned. "Dwayne."

Opal came out on the porch and called everyone in for dinner. Ricky and L. Dog ran up the steps and through the living room, bumping the display cabinet that held Opal's Hummel figurines.

"What I tell you boys about running in the house?" Hurley said.

He took his seat at the head of the table, Buddy beside him. Opal sat at the far end of the table. He said the blessing.

After the amens, he passed around the pot roast and carrots. Opal served her baked apples and Leanne her potato-cheese casserole. He hated the way Leanne chewed her food, pushing her lips forward with every bite.

"What did y'all think of that sermon today?" Opal said. "I always loved the tale of the Good Samaritan."

"I can never get it straight about who the Samaritans were," Dawn said.

"They were descended of the Israelites," Leanne said. "The other Jews looked down on them, but not Jesus."

Dwayne blurted out. "Jesus was a Jew?"

"Yes, he was a Jew," Leanne said. "He developed his own set of teachings and Christianity is based on those. The moral is you never know who might help you out in life. It could be someone you least suspect."

She glanced at Hurley. He glared back. Was she saying he needed help? Or that *he* ought to help someone? He finished his dessert and went out on the porch.

After a time, Buddy came out and sat in the rocker beside him.

"You planning to read that Bible or are you just carrying it around to keep you company?"

Buddy fingered one of the ribbons. "I do have something to read." He opened the Bible to a marked page. "If you have put up security against your neighbor, if you have been trapped by what you said, then do this, my son, to free yourself, since you have fallen into your neighbor's hands: Go humble yourself; press your plea with your neighbor. Allow no sleep to your eyes, no slumber to your eyelids. Free yourself, like a gazelle from the hand of the hunter, like a bird from the snare of a fowler."

Hurley spat. Did anyone really expect him just to let go of his son, of the land? He'd carved a strip out of his own property like God pulled a rib from Adam. He'd *protected* his son from all those people out there who could sense the boy's weakness, who would take advantage.

He stared at the sign by the road. "Lower the price and I'll buy your house. I'll rent it to someone I know."

Buddy shook his head. "We need to get what we're asking to afford that house on Sparger."

"You leave that sign up, there's no telling who's going to buy it. Might be some nigger."

"Pa."

"You don't know!"

Chapter 5

Hurley was in the side yard spraying the dandelions when the white car came up the driveway. A woman stepped out wearing city clothes and high heels. She waved. "Pretty morning!"

From under his bush, Gus rushed out barking. The woman quick-stepped backwards, her heels wobbling on the gravel.

"Quit!" he yelled. Gus slunk away.

"I'm the realtor," the woman said. "I've got just the thing."

She reached into her purse and held out a biscuit. "Nice doggy. You be nice." Gus sniffed the biscuit, snapped it out of her hand, and carried it away.

"Buddy and Leanne aren't home," he said.

"Yes, I know. I have a key."

He bristled. They'd already given someone else a key to the house?

Another car came up the drive, a grey Buick. A bald-headed man in a sport coat and a silver-haired woman in a pink suit stepped out, nodded his way. He gave the weeds another squirt.

The realtor raised her arms wide. "Isn't it wonderful? All these big trees?"

Gus circled the group as they went around to the front door. Hurley waited until they'd gone inside, then headed back to the house.

Opal stood at the window, a twinkle in her eye. "Is Gus giving them a hard time?"

"They ought to have put him up."

"Leanne would never let Gus in the house. He'd have barked at them there."

He sat at the table while Opal fixed him a tuna sandwich. She set the plate in front of him. "I kept the pickles out of yours."

He took a bite, set the sandwich down. "Realtor lady was dressed for a party."

"I suppose that's how they do."

"Did you recognize them folks?"

"No. They don't belong to the church."

"Lots of new people in town."

The realtor and her clients came out on the back deck. She pointed out the table with the umbrella and the potted plant beneath the overhang. The man stared at the back yard, his eyes landing on the car shed and its collection of lawn mowers, gas cans, and paint buckets.

"We ought to have cleaned up our side of that shed," Opal said.

He frowned. "*We* ain't selling."

The realtor pointed back and forth between the two houses, no doubt explaining that the car shed had originally been part of Hurley's land, but was now split between the two families.

"I suppose we ought to offer to give them the middle bay," Opal said.

"They ain't gonna buy it."

"Why do you say that?"

"Couple like that don't want to share."

* * *

Over the next week, other people came to look at the house. Leanne would drive off and the realtor would arrive, followed by her clients. Hurley made a point of lingering in the yard, picking up sticks or spraying weeds. He'd give the people a hard stare, let them know who they were dealing with.

Summer came and the place still hadn't sold. Visitors dwindled with the heat. He was sitting in a rocker on the porch when Linwood Jernigan pulled up in his black sedan. Linwood was a realtor for another company and an old schoolmate. No doubt, he'd come to find out why Buddy hadn't hired him to sell the house.

"How are you doing, Hurley? I was just driving by. Saw the sign in front of Buddy's. Century 21."

"I didn't have no say in that."

"I understand. You choose whomever you're comfortable with."

With his rosy cheeks and cheerful smile, Linwood could make anyone feel you were his special friend. Hurley knew better. He nodded to the chair beside him. "Take a seat."

Linwood eased down in the chair. "Have they had anyone interested?"

"Not that I know of."

"Fifty thousand. That's high for here in the county."

"What I told him."

Linwood glanced around the hill. "Now, if these two pieces went together, that'd be a different story. Combine your twenty acres with his three and you could put in a subdivision. You could get a real good price."

"What makes you think I'd want to sell?"

"Think about it," Linwood said. "You'd never get as much for your one piece as you could with both of them together. You could get yourself a two-bedroom condo at Croasdale right on the golf course."

"I ain't a golfer."

"I know. I know. You like your lawn and garden. But let me tell you, things are going to change at this end of Hope Valley. When they put in that interchange to I-40, this here won't be farmland for long. They'll tax your property at its development value."

Hurley stared at the lawn, the cows in Marvin's meadow, the wooded ridgeline beyond. Was it really possible it could all disappear?

Linwood went on. "If you don't like the idea of a condo, I'd get a place further out in the county. Fix it up nice just like you've done here." He leaned in close, gave him a wink. "You don't want to get picked off like Buddy did. Remember that?"

Chapter 6

By the time Hurley arrived with Opal and Patsy, the bleachers on Jordan's side of the ballfield were nearly filled.

"You go on and sit with your friends," he said to Patsy. "We'll find a place."

She frowned. "What friends?"

His heart sank. Patsy had grown heavy of late. She wasn't the type to attract boys, but he'd always assumed she had some girlfriends. Truth be told, he knew almost nothing about her social life.

From the top row, Linwood waved and pointed to seats next to him and Estelle. He hesitated. Linwood's boy, Andy, was the best player on the middle school baseball team; Buddy was a bench warmer. He wasn't eager to listen to Linwood brag. But there didn't seem to be any option.

The three of them squeezed into the narrow space. Estelle leaned forward. "Is Buddy going to play today?"

"I doubt it," Opal said. "He's not been in a game yet."

"Buddy should not be playing baseball," Patsy said.

Estelle patted her knee. "Now, don't say that. Everybody ought to play something. At least try."

Hurley spotted Buddy at the far end of the bench, his big ears sticking out beneath his cap. The coach was giving the team a pep talk, while Buddy picked at his glove. Across the diamond, the Hillside team huddled by their coach. They were all coloreds, the fans in the bleachers, too. The umpire blew his whistle and Jordan took the field, Andy on the mound.

"Show 'em some heat!" Linwood shouted.

Hillside's first batter stepped to the plate.

"He looks awful big for a sixth grader," Opal said.

"They hold 'em back over there," Estelle said. "He's probably thirteen."

Linwood chuckled. "That or he can't read."

The batter sent two balls whistling foul down the third base line, firing up the coloreds in the Hillside bleachers. Andy paused and took a sign from the catcher. The next pitch seemed to stall in front of the plate. The batter swung and missed. The Jordan fans burst into applause.

"That's his screw ball," Linwood said. "I taught him that one."

Andy struck out the next two batters. Hurley shook his head. He'd never even played catch with Buddy, didn't really know how.

"Bud's uniform is just hanging off of him," Opal said. "He should have ordered a smaller size."

Hurley sniffed. "They probably gave him whatever they had left over."

On the strength of Andy's pitching and hitting, Jordan went up to an early 3-2 lead. But their catcher got injured when a Hillside player barreled into him going home. Depleted by the flu, Jordan had only three players on the bench—Carlyle, a relief pitcher, Jamie, a utility infielder, and Buddy. Coach called Jamie.

In the late innings, Hillside came on strong. They fielded with precision and scattered hits through the infield. Whenever a runner got on base, he was sure to steal before Jamie could throw him out.

In the top of the ninth, Hillside tied the game on a double, then went up by two on a home run. Jordan's coach took a tired Andy off the mound and replaced him with Carlyle.

"He did awful good," Hurley said to Linwood.

Carlyle retired the side, but it was not enough. Jordan's first two batters went down swinging. Two outs, bottom of the ninth—the end was near. The Jordan crowd fell silent, outplayed by a bunch of coloreds.

The coach looked down the length of the bench. He signaled to Buddy.

"He's putting your son in," Estelle said.

Patsy covered her head in her hands.

Buddy took some practice swings on the sideline. The bat seemed to pull him around, coming out of one of his hands at the end of each swing.

The umpire called. "Batter up!"

Buddy stepped to the plate. The first pitch was an inside fast ball that smacked into the catcher's glove before Buddy could get his bat off his shoulder.

"Strike one!"

Laughter from the stands.

"Please let this be over," Patsy said.

Intimidated by the speed of the previous pitch, Buddy backed away from the plate. The second pitch whizzed across the middle of the plate, beyond the reach of his swinging bat.

"Get up to the plate," the coach yelled. "You can't hit from outside the box."

Buddy stepped in close. The pitcher threw the next ball inside, slow enough for most players to avoid. It hit Buddy in the hand. He dropped his bat and winced in pain.

"You're on, boy. Go!" the coach yelled.

Buddy shuffled out to first base, clutching his hand. The Jordan fans cheered in jest. "Go, Buddy! Way to get on base, man."

Dane Thurber, Jordan's best hitter, was next at bat. The first base coach instructed Buddy to take a lead off the bag. The fans started to chant. Thurber swung at the first pitch, driving the ball deep to left field, just barely foul.

Rattled by Thurber's hard shot, the Hillside pitcher threw three straight balls. The catcher called for time and went out to the mound amidst a hail of boos.

"That's one thing about colored," Linwood said. "They choke when the going gets tough."

The catcher returned to home plate. The Jordan players resumed their chant. The pitcher glanced over his shoulder. Linwood yelled. "Watch yourself, Buddy!"

The pitcher spun and fired the ball to the first baseman, who tagged Buddy out as he stood five feet off the bag, looking down at his hand.

Chapter 7

Hurley never heard her arrive. He looked through the window to see a slender young woman standing in the driveway studying Buddy's empty planter. She wore a sleeveless white dress, her black hair tied in a ponytail. Gus sniffed at her bare legs. She reached down to pet him.

"Girl looking at it now," he said to Opal.

She came to the window. "She's got pretty legs."

And a nice fanny, he wanted to say. "Looks like she's been down at the beach."

"That's not a beach tan," Opal said. "She looks like a Latin person to me."

That would explain it. Not many white had fannies like that. He made note of her car, a sage green Volkswagen. "I don't see the realtor. I guess she just saw the sign and come on up."

The woman turned to reveal a beautiful face, straight nose and full lips set in a slight smile. She saw him at the window and waved.

* * *

The surveyors arrived at dawn. They pulled out their instruments, put a pin in the middle of the drive down by the road, and wrapped it with a pink ribbon. They walked past Hurley standing on the porch, not so much as a hello, and marked the pin behind the car shed. They located and marked the two corner pins over by the woods.

As soon as the surveyors left, Hurley marched down the drive and pulled the ribbon off that pin. He did the same to the pin behind the car shed. The ribbons were lying on the kitchen table when Opal came back from the grocery store.

"What have you done, now?" she asked.

"They were touching my property."

She set the groceries on the counter. "You're acting like a child. Buddy is forty-five years old. He can do what he wants."

"I do what I want."

She picked up her purse. "I'm going to the K&W."

For the first time in 50 years of marriage, Opal left him alone to make his lunch. He went to the refrigerator and opened the door. Where did she keep the sandwich fixings? After pulling out various drawers, he located the ham and cheese, the mustard and lettuce. He made the sandwich, sat down, and took a bite. Dry. He lifted the bread and realized he'd forgotten the mayonnaise. Too hungry to wait, he went on eating, tasting the dryness, pondering his actions. When he finished, he got up, went outside and put the ribbons back.

A week later, the realtor parked at the bottom of the drive, crossed the lawn and hung something on the sign. She waved at him on the porch, the winner this time, and sped away.

He steadied himself on the handrail as he descended the steps. The slope carried him down until he stood at the edge of the drive. SOLD. His head spun. Maybe he could call Buddy and offer a higher price, stop the sale from going through. Maybe call the buyers. And say what?

Opal teared up when he gave her the news. She pulled a handkerchief from her purse. “We ought to go over and talk to them as soon as Buddy gets home.”

He frowned. “You go over if you want.”

“We need to go together.”

* * *

Leanne answered the door, smiling as if nothing was wrong.

“We seen you sold the house,” Opal said.

Now, the patronizing look. “Yes, we’ve been meaning to tell you. We signed a contract three days ago.

“Who bought it?” Hurley asked. “A young couple?”

Leanne nodded. Buddy appeared wearing a guilty look. “Ma, Pa.”

“We heard the news,” Opal said. “We’re sure going to miss you.”

“We’ll miss you, too,” Leanne said. “We’ll have you over to the new place as soon as we’re moved in.”

“You already bought it?” he said.

“We closed last week.”

“When are you moving?”

“Next week. We’ve got a moving truck coming on Saturday.”

Hurley stuck out his chin. “We ain’t gonna be here to help,” he said. “We’ll be down at the beach.”

Buddy looked surprised. “You’re going to the beach?”

Leanne recognized the game and cut it short. "Hurley, the realtor said you need to move any of your stuff back to your side, so before you go, you might want to move that woodpile and any junk on our side of the car shed."

He struggled to contain his fury. Who was she to tell him what to move?

"And one more thing…" She turned to Buddy.

"We were hoping you'd look after Gus," Buddy said. "We can't have him loose over at the new place. This is where he feels at home."

He scowled. "Forget that. We ain't taking Gus."

Chapter 8

Hurley loved the drive to the beach. Behind the wheel of his Ford pick-up, the suitcases stashed beneath the camper top, he and Opal traveled through a landscape of tobacco farms and pine forests. The eastern part of North Carolina had hardly changed in the fifty years he'd been driving through. That and the pleasures of the ocean made him feel young.

At Newton Grove, they stopped at the Dairy Queen and ordered barbecue. They found a picnic table on the lawn where they could watch the cars go around the traffic circle. Opal pointed across the street where someone was hosting a sale on wooden gazebos.

"I sure would like one of those," she said. "I think it would look nice out in the yard."

He sniffed. "What's wrong with the porch?"

"A gazebo seems more romantic."

"You might get the gazebo. I ain't sure about the romance."

For the first time in a week, Opal smiled.

In mid-afternoon, they reached the trailer park, a pine-shaded tract beside the lift bridge that spanned the Intracoastal Waterway. The trailers were mostly 1950's vintage, nothing fancy. The constant thump of cars rolling on and off the bridge reminded you that those who could afford it stayed out on the island, but the trailer park had its own community.

He stepped out of the truck and breathed in the salt air. Harris called from his chair by the water. "Didn't know you were coming down this weekend."

"We decided last minute," Hurley said.

"A couple of big sailboats come by an hour ago, they had to raise the bridge. Traffic was backed up on both sides."

Opal waved. "Are a lot of people coming down for the weekend?"

"It's that construction up at the north end of the island. They're putting in a mess of condos."

They took their suitcases inside, turned on the air conditioning and opened the shades. In the kitchen, Hurley tapped down a piece of linoleum with his foot.

"Tiles come loose again," he said. "I glued that last year."

Opal frowned. "Some things won't ever stay."

He opened the sliding glass door to air out the trailer.

"You need to shut that before the bugs get in," Opal said.

He joined her in the bedroom, opened his suitcase, then got distracted by the copy of *Carolina Sportsman* he'd left on the dresser. The photos of smiling men posing beside giant marlin always whetted his appetite for deep sea fishing. He'd done that once in his life, spent a whole day on a charter boat watching his lure bounce across the waves. He caught two Spanish mackerel not twenty inches long, cost him $300.

"When do you want to eat?" he said.

"As soon as you put your clothes away."

"We ought to go before too long. People will be coming off the beach."

Opal put on a pair of capris and a sky blue Carolina T-shirt, rubbed sunscreen into her mottled arms. "I feel better, now" she said. "Are you going to change out of those work clothes?"

As the truck crested the top of the bridge, the blue line of the Atlantic came into view. Hurley couldn't remember a time when his spirits didn't rise at the sight of the ocean. This time was different. He couldn't shake the memory of why they'd come and wonder at what they'd find when they returned.

They entered the cluster of surfboard rental shops, bait stores and rental offices that passed for a town on these narrow treeless islands. The lot at the Fish House Restaurant was half full. The waitress found them a table by the window and brought a pitcher of ice tea and a basket of hush puppies.

"Like as not, that moving truck will break a few branches getting up the drive," he said.

"I just don't see how they're going to fit everything in one truck," Opal said. "They've got the two beds and dressers, all that furniture in the living room."

She ordered the small seafood plate, he the large. Neither of them could finish.

"Sparger Road," Opal said. "I know where that is, but I can't picture the house."

"It's two story with that plastic siding. I wouldn't have it."

"At least he won't have to paint."

Across the sound, the sun was setting. Purple tendrils fanned out from a distant cloud bank. "Might come a rain tomorrow."

"I hope they don't get wet."

* * *

In the morning, Opal made bacon and eggs. The fan wasn't working over the stove and the smell of bacon grease filled the trailer. Hurley suggested they take a drive over to the island to see the new development.

At the T-intersection in town, he turned north, paralleling the ocean and a line of old cinderblock cottages. The road bent away from the coast and the land turned low and swampy. This was how the island looked before all the houses went up—clumps of wax myrtle, sea oats, and live oaks, their tops flattened by the wind. It was a reminder of how hard life was here much of the time.

They curved back toward the beach and the condominiums came into view, big cubes on stilts jammed right against the frontal dune. The road ended in a cul-de-sac. He parked the truck and sauntered up to a man in a hard hat staring at a set of plans.

"You the builder?" Hurley said.

The man nodded.

"How much are these going for?"

"$500,000 for a three-bedroom."

He whistled. "That's too much for a working man."

"There's nothing going up on this island for a working man. It's all high-end."

"Those are mighty close to the water," Opal said. "Seems like a good storm'll wash 'em away."

The builder frowned. "The pilings are sunk down eight feet. They aren't going anywhere."

Beyond the cul-de-sac, a sand flat tapered to a cut where the seawater rushed through.

"Last time we were here, that cut was way up yonder," Hurley said. "It's come this way about a hundred yards."

The man ignored him.

"I'm going back to the truck," Opal said. "It makes me feel queer."

He was glad to get back to town with its old stucco stores and motels. They'd been here for 50 years on what passed for high ground. They wouldn't be gone any time soon.

"How about a walk on the pier?" he said.

Opal smiled. "That'd be nice."

They parked in the sand lot and climbed the wooden steps to the pier house. Melvin Swopes sat behind the counter, his black beard gone to salt-and pepper. He greeted him and Opal, asked if he could fix them up with some rods.

"We're just here for a walk," Opal said.

Melvin smiled. "Keep an eye on that husband of yours."

Through the double screen door, the sun glinted off the ocean. The waves swept across the wide beach with a soothing hiss. He and Opal walked down the pier. Halfway out, they ran into Charley Mangum tending his rod.

"Thought you weren't coming down until next week, Hurley," Charley said. "Your lawn mower must have run out of gas."

"Buddy and Leanne are moving out this weekend," Opal said. "We'd just as soon not be around."

Charley shook his head. "Kin don't ever do how you'd like 'em to." He reeled his line in to check his bait. "Why don't you two pick up a rod? Set down and relax."

Hurley looked in Charley's bucket. "Don't look like you're having much luck."

"You're too impatient. That's why you'll never make a good fisherman."

He sniffed. "I was catching fish before you were born."

"You weren't doing nothing but shittin' in your britches before I was born. Pardon the language, Opal."

She laughed. "You got that right."

They walked on to the end of the pier, where three men dressed in dark, heavy jackets leaned against the rail. Their lines ran far out beyond the breaking waves. Hurley eyed their sleeping bags and empty food wrappers. King mackerel fishermen. They'd been here all night.

"Catching anything?" he said.

"Nah."

He watched the waves slide by, the water rising and falling around the wooden pillars. It seemed like there were fewer big fish these days, people waiting longer and longer for something to bite. But the sight of these men out here taking a chance stirred his blood.

Back in the trailer, he pulled his tackle box out of the closet. He sat at the kitchen table and tried to untangle the assortment of line, weights, and hooks. "You straighten these things out, come back a week later and they're all a mess. How does that happen?"

"I guess they shift around in the box," Opal said.

"Who shifts them? I don't."

Opal sat on the couch sorting through a jar of shells she'd collected on the last trip. She held each one against a wooden frame, threw the rejects into the wastebasket.

"I don't know as I want to do this today," she said.

He looked out the window. There were still about four hours of daylight left, just enough time to get back to Durham. "Let's go home."

* * *

The sun was down by the time they pulled into the drive. Hurley pointed to a branch dangling from one of the overhanging trees.

"I told you that truck wouldn't clear that oak."

"Looks like they took the curtains," Opal said.

At the top of the drive, Gus came out from under his bush.

"Oh, Lord. They must have left him," Opal said.

"He won't be left for long."

Gus approached as he stepped out from the truck.

"Git!"

They walked over to Buddy and Leanne's deck and cupped their hands against the sliding glass door.

Opal pulled her head away. "They're gone."

Chapter 9

Hurley was reading the paper in the kitchen when a U-Haul truck pulled up. "Here they are," Opal said.

He set the paper down and joined Opal at the window. A curly-headed man stepped down from the driver's seat, the dark-haired girl beside him. They looked at the house and hugged.

"That must be the husband," Opal said.

"Don't get too close, now."

A foreign station wagon and a small pickup arrived. Two men got out of the pick-up, a heavy-set person and a tall, thin colored.

"Looks like they hired some help," he said.

The colored man sauntered up, flapping his arms like a bird. He gave the dark-haired girl a hug.

"He's not acting like help," Opal said.

The man turned and looked their way.

"Get back, now," Hurley said.

Opal stepped away from the window. "I'm going to fix a chicken for dinner. Don't you have something to do?"

"I need to sharpen them mower blades."

"Well, get on, now."

He walked out the back door, past the line of sheds, and through the open bay doors of the barn. In the soft, gray light, he arranged a pair of ramps in front of the John Deere and drove it forward so the front end was elevated. He grabbed a socket wrench off the bench and lay on his back, turning the bolts until the blades came loose. Then, it was back in the sunshine and over to the tool shed where he kept his grinding wheel.

The smell of motor oil greeted him as he lifted the wooden peg from the latch and opened the tool shed door. He switched on the light and scanned the walls—rake, hoe, shovel, ax, mattock, saw, post-hole digger—two of each. People made fun of him for having duplicates, but wouldn't it be their luck to break a shovel handle on a Saturday morning and have to stand in line at Lowe's?

He turned on the grinding wheel and centered his goggles. Sparks flew from the blade as he held it to the wheel. Most people took their mower blades for granted, let them get dull until the grass was shredded more than cut. He knew better. Inch by inch, the cutting edge took on a silver sheen.

He reattached the blades to the mower and went back to the house. As he came through the door, he saw Opal looking out the side window.

"I caught you, girl," he said.

"I was just taking a peek."

"I bet you've been standing there the whole time."

"I have not. I've been fixing this chicken."

He joined her at the window. "What are they up to now?"

"I think they're about done. I haven't seen them out at the truck in awhile."

"Colored boy do any more hugging?"

"No. He and the other fella carried a mattress out of the truck. I didn't see any bed frame."

"They might just lay it on the floor."

Opal waved her hand. "I don't know what young people do these days."

* * *

In the morning after the dew was gone from the grass, Hurley and Opal waded into the garden. He paused before a promising-looking ear of corn, and parted the silken hairs to find the kernels glowing soft yellow. He snapped the ear off, dropped it in the basket, and moved on down the row.

"Is two enough?" he asked.

Opal looked up from her tomatoes. "Pick four. They might want to do a few things with them."

He moved on to the green beans, picking a couple of quarts.

"Should we put everything in one bag?" he asked.

"No, you don't want to bruise the tomatoes by mixing it up."

After rinsing the vegetables in the outdoor sink, he and Opal crossed the drive. He knocked on the side door, peeked through the curtained window. "She's running the vacuum."

"We might ought to come back."

He knocked again and the vacuum shut off. "Here she comes."

The door opened to reveal a slender, dark-haired woman, a head taller than Opal. She wore a sleeveless shirt and cut-off jeans. The black crescent of her eyebrows was so finely shaped it looked to have been trimmed. Her skin was cocoa-colored, kind of Spanish.

"I'm Hurley. This here's Opal. We've come to introduce ourselves."

She broke into an easy smile.

"We've been hoping to meet you," she said. "My name's Renata."

She extended her hand, soft as a cow's udder, and called over her shoulder, "Danny, come meet the neighbors."

A stocky figure with round shoulders strode into the room, short brown hair, small mouth, breasts.

"Hey, there. I'm Danny."

She shook his hand with a firm grip. Danny was a woman. And not just any woman. She was the one he'd seen hit by the egg at the lesbian parade.

Opal looked confused. "Are you two friends?"

Renata smiled. "Yes, we are."

"I thought there was another one here."

"No, it's just the two of us."

"Well..." Opal held had out her bag. "We brought you some vegetables."

Renata peered inside. "Oh, my gosh, did you grow these?"

"That's our garden over by the barn," Opal said.

Hurley offered his bag to Danny.

"Wow, those are some good looking tomatoes," Danny said.

He felt a moment of relief. At least, she knew something about vegetables.

"We really want to have a garden," Renata said. "We've been wondering where to put it, but there are so many trees around the house."

She gestured at the big oaks overhead. Was she thinking of cutting one down? He was about to speak when Opal gave him a warning glance.

"Buddy said you're both retired," Danny said.

"Five years," Hurley said. "We both worked at American Tobacco. How about you?"

"I'm a lab technician at The National Institutes of Health," Renata said. "It's over in the Research Park."

"Our daughter-in-law, she works over in the Park," Opal said. "She's a receptionist at IBM."

"That's right down the street."

"And I teach religion at Duke," Danny said.

Opal brightened. "That's nice. What church do you go to?"

"We don't really have a church."

"Oh, uh huh."

He hoped Opal would leave it at that, but she kept right on.

"We belong to Mount Moriah Baptist Church," she said. "We'd love for you to come visit."

Danny glanced at Renata. "I'm not sure we'd fit in."

"Why's that?"

"Renata and I are a couple."

The color drained from Opal's face. Her eyes lost focus. Hurley held onto his smile, waiting a polite interval before putting his hand on her shoulder.

"We're gonna head on back," he said. "You need anything, give us a holler."

Chapter 10

In the kitchen, Hurley sat at the table working a toothpick between his teeth. Opal ran her knife down the corn cobs, smacking the blade into the cutting board.

"How was I to know?" she said. "I thought they might just be friends."

"You can tell by looking," he said. "The pretty one's the woman. The other's the man."

"And her teaching religion. How do they allow it?"

"That's Duke."

Opal carried the bag of corn into the mud room and put it in the chest freezer.

"I'm opposed to it. It's not natural."

"I see Marvin's heifers do it all the time. One jumping up on the other."

"That's cows." She stared out the window. "I worry about Ricky and Little Dwayne. What are we going to tell them?"

"Say they're friends, just like you thought."

"I know Dwayne's going to say something smart."

* * *

When he and Opal arrived home from church, Danny and Renata were kneeling at the top of the driveway, petting Gus. "What are going to do about the dog?" she said.

"I'll feed him, but I ain't taking him in."

"You'd better ask them."

He parked the Oldsmobile in the car shed and stepped into the driveway.

"Is this your dog?" Danny said.

"That's Gus, Buddy's dog," he said. "Is he bothering you?"

"Not at all. Is Buddy coming back to get him?"

"He left him. They don't want him at the new house."

Renata rubbed the dog's ears. "Poor Gus. You've been abandoned."

He pointed to the Acuba bush at the corner of the ranch house. "I'll feed him, but he's like to stay under that bush."

Danny looked at Renata. "That's fine," Renata said. "You'll be our dog, won't you, Gus?"

Hurley lingered. "Another thing, Opal parks her car in the left side of the shed. Right side's yours. We can talk about the middle."

"We never keep our cars in a garage," Danny said. "You can take them both."

He nodded. "The realtor tell you we share the driveway? It needs to be graded and graveled every couple of years. Buddy works for a landscaping contractor. He brings his grader over here and gives us a good price."

"Sounds like a deal," Danny said. She pointed to the woodpile in her backyard. "Who's is that?"

"That's mine. I'll move it tomorrow. What are you planning to do about your yard?"

Danny stared at the grass, now past ankle height. She pointed at the push mower by the shed. “Well…I’ve got that thing.”

He scoffed. “You aim to cut your whole yard with that? I’d get me a rider.”

“A riding lawn mower?”

“That’s right.”

“We hadn’t counted on buying something like that,” Renata said.

He gave his little smile. “There’s a lot you don’t count on in life. Sometimes you’ve got to adjust.”

Chapter 11

Opal's Sunday pork loin was extra good. She'd put in slivers of garlic, served it up with applesauce and sour cream mashed potatoes. Hurley had just finished a second helping when Leanne asked what he and Opal thought of the new neighbors.

"We haven't had much chance to talk with them," Opal said. "We took them over some vegetables. They seemed right friendly."

Dwayne smirked. "For lesbos."

Buddy frowned. "Dwayne!"

Ricky looked up from his plate. "What's lesbos?"

Leanne sighed. "Dawn, will you take those boys outside?"

When the boys were gone, she apologized. "Honestly, we want to know how you all are getting along. We didn't have a say in who bought the house."

"What did I tell you about selling?" he said.

"Maybe they'll turn out to be fine. You never know about people."

"Too bad Aunt Patsy ain't around," Dwayne said.

Opal looked up. "What do you mean by that?"

Dwayne shrugged, made a stupid face.

Hurley wiped his mouth. "I'm going out on the porch."

He sunk into his rocker and pulled out a chaw of Red Man. Dawn had taken the boys over to the garden to hunt tomato worms. They yipped like coyotes when they found one, smashed them on the ground with chunks of dirt. He stared across the drive at the neighbor's yard, imagined what his friends were saying. "Are those girls gonna let the hill go wild? Have a hippie ceremony?"

Leanne and Buddy came out on the porch. She touched his shoulder. "We're headed out. I apologize for what happened."

He waved them away.

The guests got into their cars and headed down the road, the sound of the tires fading into the distance. Across the way, Marvin's cows moved in slow motion across the pasture. He couldn't think about those two women without picturing the sex act. Why would the pretty one want to be with the other? Was Danny good with her tongue? Did she know how to work one of those dildos?

He spat into his can, listened for Opal. She usually came out on the porch after the family left. He watched the cars passing on the road, stragglers coming home from Sunday dinner. Two bike riders peddled by in tight yellow shirts. That was something you never used to see.

Finally, he got up and went inside. Opal wasn't in the kitchen. Not in the laundry. He found her in the bedroom, gazing at Patsy's picture on the wall.

"You feeling tired?" he asked.

"I was just thinking."

"You don't have to fix me supper. I'll just eat leftovers."

"Good, because I wasn't planning on cooking you anything."

He looked up. "Did I say something to make you mad?"

"You didn't say anything. That's the problem. You left me alone in the middle of that conversation."

"Dwayne ought to have kept his mouth shut," he said.

Opal wiped away a tear. "He might have been right for once. She might have made friends with those two. We'll never know."

Chapter 12

Opal had the feeling that Hurley was working himself up to something. He'd been making eyes at her in the hallway, passing notes to his tenth grade friends. Susan Hadden kidded Opal about her "big-eared boyfriend," but Opal thought he had a nice smile. He wasn't handsome like the country club crowd. None of them were. They were the children of farmers and mill workers, with pocked skin and crooked teeth.

She *was* frustrated that Hurley wouldn't stop and speak to her. She was too shy to make her own approach. And so they continued this game of glances. Then one Saturday morning, Opal's mother called from the kitchen to say Hurley was in the yard on a horse.

Opal set down her book and walked out the porch steps. Hurley sat atop a white gelding, his long legs draped over the horse's back. "Hey, Opal. I come to see if you wanted to ride up to the rhododendron bluffs. We could go wading."

Opal had heard about the bluffs on New Hope Creek. People talked about them as if they were a different world. She heard that boys drank beer and smoked cigarettes, went skinny dipping in the creek. She held her hand out to the horse's muzzle asking, "What's your horse's name?"

"King."

She felt his steamy breath. "I'll have to ask Momma."

Annie Mae hesitated at Opal's request. Hurley Cates wasn't of the class that she would hope for her daughter, but he seemed to be a nice enough boy.

"You be careful around those rocks," she said.

Hurley helped Opal onto King's back. Her short legs barely reached King's midsection, but she loved the warmth of the horse's body on her thighs.

"Hold on, now," he said.

She wrapped her arms around Hurley's stomach, felt the firmness of his muscles. His T-shirt smelled of laundry detergent. "How did you get here?" she asked.

"Up Chapel Hill Road."

"Your parents let you ride there?"

"This is the furthest I've come."

They clopped along the hard top, birds singing in the trees, the scent of honeysuckle wafting from the meadow.

Susan's house came into view. Opal couldn't wait for her to see this. Sheeba came barking across the lawn, causing King to shy. Susan's brother, Larry, looked out from his miniature log cabin.

"Larry, get Sheeba!" Opal yelled.

Larry took the dog into the house. A minute later, Susan came out the front door, a wry smile on her face.

"We're going up to the rhododendron bluffs," Hurley said. "You ought to come along."

Susan looked around. "Is anyone with you?"

Hurley shook his head.

"We'll be back through in a little while," Opal said.

Hurley turned onto Whitfield Road and kicked King into a trot. Opal's breasts jostled against Hurley's back. She leaned away.

At the top of the hill, Hurley cut onto a path that ran through a tract of recently-timbered forest. There was nothing left but stumps and broomsage.

"I wish they hadn't cut this," Opal said.

Hurley shrugged. "It weren't nothing but pines."

The path sloped down through a hardwood forest. Opal sensed they were near the creek, but the valley kept dropping. Finally, Hurley pulled King to a halt. He helped Opal down and tied King's reins to a tree.

"We've got to walk from here," he said. "Mind when we get out on the rocks."

They approached a band of dark green rhododendron. Hurley parted the branches like a curtain to a stage. When Opal stepped out onto the rock, she was looking down at the tops of the trees.

"It makes me dizzy," she said.

Hurley grinned. "I told you."

He picked up a rock and tossed it straight out. For long seconds, it spun through the air, slapping at last into the creek.

"Come on sit down," Hurley said.

Without asking, he stripped off his shirt. His chest was disappointingly flat, but the muscles on his belly made her tingle. He looked at her with a goofy smile.

"You got pretty eyes," he said. "I like they way they turn down at the ends."

Opal blushed. She didn't know what she was supposed to do next. Should she compliment his smile? Kiss him?

Hurley stood. "Let's wade in the stream."

"I don't have a suit."

"You can just go in your shorts. They'll be dry time we get back."

Hurley led the way down the bluff, pointing out the handholds in the rock. It was like climbing down a ladder, but scarier for the unevenness of the steps. Opal felt she might fall at any moment.

Finally, they were down. Hurley stepped into the creek. She followed, wading out until the water was up to her waist. "It's cold!"

"No, it ain't."

She had never done such a crazy thing in her life. Hurley brought her alongside and together they waded down the middle of the stream as if they owned the world.

At a bend in the creek, Hurley told her to wait. He waded toward a fallen tree that lay against the bank, leaned over and started feeling his way along the bottom.

"What are you doing?"

Hurley didn't answer, just kept moving along the bank. Suddenly, he stopped. The water rippled beside him.

"Oh, man, it's a big one."

He raised his arm. Something big and black was stuck on the end. A catfish! He lifted the fish clear of the water, its enormous mouth engulfing Hurley's hand. "Woo hoo!" Hurley cried. "A five pounder!"

The catfish let go and disappeared with a splash. Hurley waded toward her, shaking his hand.

"Oh, my gosh," Opal said. "It's bleeding!"

"It's alright. They don't have no teeth."

"How did you know that fish was there?"

"I felt him. Catfish come up from the lake in the spring. They like to make a nest under a log."

"And you let him bite you?"

Hurley grinned. "That's how you catch 'em. They won't let go once they get ahold of something."

Wading back up the stream, Opal composed the story she would tell Susan. "Hurley was so brave, he didn't even cry out. He just let that fish bite down."

She was out of breath by the time they scaled the bluff. Hurley turned to help her up the last incline. He had a funny look in his eye. Before she could speak, he kissed her.

"And I didn't care that he smelled like catfish," she told Susan. "I just knew that he was in love with me."

Chapter 13

Hurley was spraying dandelions when Danny and Renata came out in the back yard. They looked up at the trees, then down at the ground. They got out a tape measure and started taking measurements. Despite Opal's warnings, he set down his sprayer and walked to middle of the drive.

Renata greeted him. "We're trying to figure out where to put our fall garden. It's awfully shady back here. We were wondering about taking down some of these trees."

"I wouldn't do that if I was you," he said. "Trees keep the house cool."

"There's always the front yard," Danny said.

"You don't want to tear up your lawn."

They stood for awhile, looking around the yard.

"Tell you what," he said, "I've got an old tobacco field out yonder. I'm of a mind to plant my corn there next summer. That'd be a good place to put your garden. Lot's of sun. The soil's already loose."

Renata stared at the path disappearing into the woods. "How far is it?" she said.

"Not too far."

* * *

In the evening, Hurley walked out to the barn and climbed atop the tractor. He pulled out the starter button, then the starter rod. The engine thrummed to life. He backed over to the lean-to and hitched up the wagon. Then, he drove to the tool shed to pick up wooden stakes, a hammer and a hoe.

Renata and Danny were waiting in the back yard, Gus wagging beside them. He shut the engine off and nodded at the wagon.

"Lower that gate and you can set yourselves down in the back."

Danny walked around to the front of the tractor and ran her hands along the cowling. "A Farmall Super A. What year is this, 1945?"

"'46. How'd you know that?"

"My dad has a tractor."

"Is he a farmer?"

"He's a builder. But we have a fair amount of land in north Durham. He likes to keep it mowed."

"You're from Durham?"

"From out in the county. Does that surprise you?"

He wouldn't say so, but it did surprise him that there was a family from Durham with a lesbian for a daughter.

"Y'all pull your legs up. Mind the start."

He pulled down on the throttle and the tractor lurched forward. The women teetered backwards, righted themselves and laughed. These were some good time gals.

With Gus running in front, he steered the tractor into the tunnel of green. Big twisty oaks filtered the sunlight into bright flashes. The air felt five degrees cooler. He'd thought of timbering this woods a number of times, but the older the trees got, the less he felt inclined. The trees were like old friends.

The path opened onto the field, tinted gold in the evening light. He drove into the tall grass and shut the tractor off. The quiet rushed in.

"Wow, do you own all this?" Renata said.

"Over to them pines."

"It's beautiful."

He studied the pale meadow grass and the orange broomsage covering the old dirt rows. It was just an overgrown field, but maybe it looked natural to a city girl.

"You used to grow tobacco?" Danny said.

"Ten years ago. It was hard to keep after it and work a factory job at the same time."

She kicked at the ground, picked up a chunk of dirt. "That's some red clay. We'll need to add fertilizer."

"But no chemicals," Renata said.

"Can we get some cow manure from Marvin?" Danny asked.

"If you want to shovel it."

"That would be great."

He took the stakes out of the wagon and pounded one in the ground. "I'm going to put my garden right here. You can put yours beside it. How big are you planning to make it?"

Renata took a piece of paper out of her pocket and unfolded it. "I'm thinking two rows of collards, a row of beets, a row of Brussel sprouts, and a row of broccoli."

"Broccoli?"

"You don't like broccoli?"

"Nah."

"It's good for you. It's full of anti-oxidants. They help prevent cancer."

"Cancer?"

"Yes. You ought to think about that, especially if you use pesticides."

"I've been spraying pesticides all my life and I ain't got cancer."

"Hey, she knows," Danny said. "She feeds that stuff to rats. They get all kinds of tumors."

He stared at Renata. "How you aiming to keep the bugs away?"

"Marigolds," she said. "You plant them between the vegetables. Bugs don't like the smell."

He shook his head. "You girls do what you want. I'm spraying mine."

"You can call us women," Danny said. "We crossed that line about 15 years ago."

He banged in the stakes, the women's silence louder than his hammer.

"I've got something I ain't told you," he said. "I saw y'all at the parade downtown."

Both of the women looked up, their faces gone pale. "I thought that was you," Danny said. "You were carrying a sign."

"Me and Opal came with the church. The Reverend give the signs to us."

"Were you the one that threw the egg?"

"No. But I know who did."

"That was some bullshit, man."

He winced. No woman had ever talked to him that way.

They worked on in silence. Renata took out her tape measure and started laying a row. He picked up the end and stretched it out for her to mark. When enough time had passed, he broached the subject that had been on his mind.

"What are y'all planning to do about your lawn?"

Danny stood up. "I guess we're going to have to buy a rider. We'll see what we can afford."

"I can help you with that," he said. "They've got a senior discount down at Colvard's. I can buy the mower for you and you give me a check."

"You'd do that for us?"

He nodded.

"Wow, that's really nice."

He finished pounding the stakes and stood up to stretch his back. For the first time since Buddy had announced he was leaving, he felt light-hearted. His confession to the women was a weight off his shoulders. And their plans to buy a rider was icing on the cake. Maybe things were going to work out after all.

* * *

By the time Hurley got back to the house, Opal was in the living room watching her *Miami Vice*. She muted the sound.

"What in the world took you so long?"

"We were laying out the rows."

"I was starting to worry."

He smiled. "Did you think they were going to rough me up?"

"I didn't know what to think."

He sat in his recliner and took out his Red Man. Opal turned sideways to see his face.

"Well, what were they like?"

"The women? They're pretty regular."

"Regular?"

He worked the tobacco into his cheek. "That Renata thinks we ought to be planting broccoli. Said it prevents cancer."

"Oh?"

"Said she doesn't want to use any pesticides either."

"How are they planning to keep the bugs away?"

"She's planting marigolds."

"Marigolds?"

"They've got all kinds of crazy notions."

The show came back on. He reached for the remote and turned up the sound. When the next ad came on, Opal took back the remote and turned it down.

"Did you talk to them about the lawn?" she asked.

He nodded. "They decided to buy a rider. I told 'em I'd take 'em on down to Colvard's, help them pick one out."

Opal looked over. "I thought they couldn't afford a riding lawn mower."

"I said I'd put it on my tab, get that senior discount."

"You're going to buy it for them?"

"They'll write me a check afterwards."

Opal's stare burned a hole in the side of his cheek. It felt a little scary having gone out on a limb. He reached for the remote and turned up the sound.

Chapter 14

A light breeze rose up the hill, ruffling the sheets as Opal clipped them to the clothes line. It seemed like there was always a breeze in the morning. Hurley said it was because of the difference in temperature between the bottom down near Marvin's and the land up here in the sun. The wind was like a little spirit that stopped to say hello.

The door opened across the drive and Renata stepped out with a tray of small orange flowers. She set the tray on the drive and studied the brick planter.

"I thought you were gone downtown with Hurley," Opal said.

"There wasn't much room in the truck," Renata said. "And Danny's the one that knows about mowers."

Opal nodded. "Oh, uh-huh."

"It's nice today, isn't it?" Renata said.

"There was a breeze a minute ago."

Gus came out from under his bush and sniffed Renata's bare legs. Opal thought how nice it would be to wear shorts again. These days, she didn't have the kind of legs you wanted to show off.

"Are you putting in some flowers?" She asked.

"Yes, the planter looks kind of barren."

"Buddy put that planter in for Leanne. She never did anything with it. What kind of flowers are those?"

"Portulacas," Renata said. "They're a kind of succulent."

"A succulent?"

"Like a cactus. They don't need a lot of water."

"That overhang blocks the rain. You'll need to water it every once in awhile."

She caught herself. This was the kind of thing Hurley did, giving advice when it wasn't asked for. She turned back to the laundry.

"I wonder how Hurley and Danny are faring?" Renata said.

She was pleased Renata had spoken again. "They're probably doing alright," she said. "Hurley loves to talk about mowers."

"Danny's pretty mechanical, too."

"That's unusual for a girl."

A voice inside urged her not to say anything more. The other said speak. "We had a daughter who was like that."

"Oh, is she still around?"

"No. She decided to leave us some time back."

Renata stopped her work. "She died?"

"Yes." Opal's eyes welled up. "It was about fifteen years ago. 1970."

"What happened?"

"She committed suicide. We aren't sure why. She didn't have many friends."

"I'm so sorry. That must have been awful for you and Hurley."

"It's been right hard. She was Hurley's favorite. They loved to do things together. Fixing motors and such."

She hadn't talked to anyone about Patsy in a long time. It felt good to speak her name. Patsy would have liked these women. They'd have had things to talk about.

"We still have Buddy," she said.

Renata smiled. "He seems like a nice man."

"He's had his own trouble. He used to get picked on by the boys at school. Hurley felt he had to protect him. That's why he built him this house."

"Is that's why it's so close to yours?"

"Uh huh. Though I don't think you can really protect a child. You end up doing as much harm as good. That's why he and Leanne moved away. They were tired of Hurley bothering them all the time."

She pulled out a pair of Hurley's boxer shorts and pinned them on the line. For a moment, she felt self-conscious, as if she was revealing some part of him that ought to be kept private. But Renata was already back at work, setting plants in the ground.

"We feel really lucky to have gotten this place," Renata said. "We've driven by here for years imagining what it would be like on this hill."

"Is that right?"

Renata nodded. "Everybody does."

Opal laughed. "It's not all happy times."

"I'm sure. Anyway, I hope you'll find us good neighbors."

Opal finished pinning up the laundry. She picked up her basket and started for the house. "If Hurley gets too nosey, you tell him. He has a habit of messing in other people's business."

"Oh, he's no bother," Renata said.

"Well…you two haven't been here that long."

Chapter 15

Hurley wasn't sure what to say, driving down Hope Valley Road with a lesbian sitting beside him. He stared out the window, watched the scattered bungalows gave way to mansions shaded with big pines and oaks. A golf cart crossed the road, carrying a foursome onto the fairway of the Hope Valley Country Club.

"You play golf?" he asked.

"I did when I was young," Danny said. "My dad used to take me to Hillandale."

He pointed to the clubhouse at the bottom of the hill. "You ought to join up. Hope Valley."

"Somehow, I doubt they'd admit me."

He laughed. "They wouldn't let me in either."

They passed from Hope Valley into the Duke Forest neighborhood. The university bell tower rose above the pines.

"Do you like working for Duke?" he said.

"It's alright. I'd like it a lot better if I could get tenure."

"They can't fire you then. Ain't that right?"

"That's pretty much right. And the pay is a lot better."

He nodded. "Do you have a nice office?"

"Pretty nice. It's right off the Quad."

"Where's that?"

"Right under that bell tower. You've never seen the Quad?"

He shook his head.

"Take a left here," Danny said. "I'll show you."

They rounded a circle and headed up a drive bordered by huge magnolias. The belltower loomed like the Temple of Oz.

Danny pointed to a stone building beside an immaculate lawn shaded by big willow oaks. "That's my building right there. Third floor."

"Looks like a movie place."

"There's plenty of drama."

"How do you mean?"

"Office politics."

He didn't understand exactly, but decided not to pursue the subject. A tall blonde walked past with a notebook tucked under her arm. "Looks like a cheerleader there."

Danny laughed. "Do you come to many games?"

"I go to football. I can't get me a ticket to basketball."

"You need to come to a women's basketball game," she said.

He cocked his head. "Women's?"

"Hey, we're good. And we've got cheerleaders."

They left campus and drove onto the downtown expressway. At the crest of the hill, the downtown came into view—a humble skyline of old office towers. Hurley pointed to the brick factory running the length of Blackwell Street. "That's where I used to work. American Tobacco. It's all closed up now."

"What did you do?"

"I ran the blending machine."

"You made sure those cigarettes had enough nicotine?"

"I didn't know nothin' about that."

"I'll bet."

A water tower with a faded Lucky Strike logo loomed above the shuttered complex.

"I read someone's thinking of converting that into apartments," Danny said.

He sniffed. "Who wants to live downtown? Ain't nothin' but a bunch of niggers."

"What did you say?"

He fell silent. It was frustrating to have to watch how you talked around young people these days. They had no idea what things had been like. It was a different town back then, a different time.

* * *

With the night shift getting off, workers streamed out the doors of American Tobacco. Hurley and Opal passed them in the parking lot, nodding at familiar faces—coloreds, whites, men, and women. Inside the factory, they went their separate ways. He worked upstairs in the blending operation. Different brands of cigarettes used different blends of tobacco, with fillers mixed in and additives sprayed on. He had no idea what all was in the blends—that was a company secret. His job was to take the shredded tobacco as it came off the belt and spread it evenly in a tub with a pitchfork. When the tub was full, a man pushed it on rollers into an elevator to go downstairs to be rolled and cut into cigarettes. Opal worked on the first floor at the end of a conveyor belt where the freshly cut cigarettes tumbled into a tray and were fed into packs. If any of the cigarettes faced the wrong way, Opal straightened them out.

At the stairway, he joined the other day shift workers heading up to the fifth floor. Ruben, the colored man who worked the tubs on his line, climbed beside him.

"You go to the Bulls last night?" Hurley asked.

Ruben nodded. "Oh, yeah. Saw you and your family. Your girl's getting all grown up."

"She caught a foul ball last week."

"With her bare hands?"

Hurley beamed. "Reached right up and grabbed it."

At the top of the stairs, he punched in and walked down the windowless factory floor. The smell of fresh-cut tobacco mixed with the hum of machinery. A.C., the night shift worker, lowered his pitchfork.

"It's all yours," A.C. said. "I'm going home to get some sleep. You and Ruben can let the girls in."

Hurley laughed. "I already done the girls. Just left your house."

He took the pitchfork from A.C. and set to work spreading the tobacco as it came off the belt and dropped into the tub. It was an easy job, some might say boring, but it beat working outside. The big overhead fans kept you cool, the steady thrum of the machines soothed your mind. Come lunch time, you went to the cafeteria and helped yourself to a big plate of barbecue and a glass of ice tea. There was always a friendly crowd talking about baseball or basketball, passing around the latest joke. Only this year, there was a new line of conversation.

The Supreme Court had passed a law saying it was unconstitutional to have separate facilities for colored and white. Up until now, colored and white had gotten along pretty well in Durham. The working people were mostly Democrats. They'd voted in a mayor who got along with colored. But with this new law, people were afraid that the schools would be integrated schools. That was going too far.

As Hurley stood outside during a cigarette break, he was approached by Jack Ingram, an organizer for a new voting group,

Citizens for something. Ingram asked about his family. Then he brought up the desegregation ruling, *Brown versus Education.*

"We've got to put a stop to this and the place to start is local," Ingram said. "Mayoral and council elections are coming up in November. We need to vote Edwards and them out and put in some people with common sense."

Hurley hesitated. "Seems like Edwards has done pretty good so far."

Ingram leaned in close. He nodded toward Ruben and the other coloreds leaned against the wall laughing and cutting up. "Do you want to risk having niggers in school with your own? Imagine one of them kissing your Patsy. And Buddy. Those boys get around him, he's like to get roughed up real bad."

Hurley was already worried about Buddy. He was getting picked on by the bigger boys. He needed all the help he could get.

"Are you with us or against us?" Ingram said. "You've got to choose."

"Oh, I'm with you."

* * *

Hurley and Danny came off the expressway and turned north on Foster Street. They passed a row of tobacco warehouses, boarded up now just like the factories. Ever since the government had turned against cigarettes, the city had been in decline and there wasn't any reason to believe it was going to turn around. Colvard's was one of the last businesses in this part of town, a cinderblock building with a yellowed display window showing bags of grass seed.

The door bell jangled as they stepped inside. A large man in coveralls glanced up from behind the counter. "Hurley Cates."

"J.P."

"Be with you in a minute."

The wooden showroom floor was packed with lawn mowers, seeders, and tillers. On a calendar behind the counter, a buxom blonde in leather shorts rode a chainsaw.

Colvard emerged from behind the counter. "This your cousin?"

Hurley grinned. "She's my neighbor."

"What can I do for you?"

Danny explained that they were looking for a riding lawn mower—"nothing too expensive."

Colvard motioned toward a row of lime green lawn tractors. "John Deere's your best rider. It's not the cheapest, but it's the best."

Danny approached the line of mowers. She eased into one of the bright yellow seats. "It's huge."

"How big's your yard?" Colvard asked.

"I don't know. Two acres?"

Hurley nodded. "Runs upside a hill."

"You're gonna want something with some horsepower. That one's got it."

Danny lifted a price tag. "Jeez. A thousand dollars?"

"Show her the Murrays," Hurley said.

Colvard steered them to the line of red mowers. "Murray's a good mower. We've got 'em starting at 12 horsepower on up to a 21."

"Twelve is probably plenty," Danny said.

"You might want to go with the fourteen. That's mid-range."

She played with the throttle. "How much is this one?"

"Five hundred."

She raised the mowing deck up and down, fiddled with the throttle. "I don't know. They've got that 14 horsepower at Sears for four-fifty. You know, that one you liked, Hurley?"

"What's that? Oh, yeah, the Sears. That's a good mower."

Colvard went back to the counter and scratched some numbers on a pad. "I can give this one to you for four-fifty."

"Sounds like a deal," Danny said.

Hurley stepped in. "You still offering that senior discount?"

Colvard frowned. "I thought she was the one that's buying?"

"No, I'm paying for it."

Colvard rang up the register. "Four-twenty-five. With the senior discount."

Chapter 16

Hurley parked by the car shed and unhinged the tailgate to the wagon. He and Danny laid out a pair of boards as ramps and rolled the bright red mower onto the drive.

Renata came out of the house. "Wow, look at that!"

"It's a Murray," Danny said. "Fourteen horsepower."

Hurley pointed to the hinged deflector attached to the mowing deck. "First thing I'd do is take that shield off."

"Are you serious?" Danny said. "That's there to keep it from throwing out rocks and stuff."

"If you want to mow close to those trees, you need to take that off. That's what I did with mine."

Renata knit her brow. "Isn't that like a government regulated safety feature?"

He smiled. "Government tries to make you do a lot of things. That there is for people who've got no sense to stand beside a running lawn mower."

Danny arrived with the toolbox. She lay on the ground and backed out the screws until the deflector dropped to the ground. She stood and tossed it aside.

"Now, tilt that seat forward," he said. "There's a wire goes to a cut-off switch. Any time you raise out of that seat, it'll shut the engine off. I like to keep mine running."

Renata rolled her eyes. "I'm going inside."

Danny found the connector and pulled it apart. Hurley smiled. "Now, you're ready."

With a turn of the key, the engine roared to life. Danny put the mower in gear and headed for the front lawn.

"Run it in third!" He watched her mow down to the road, then headed inside for lunch.

Opal set his sandwich on the table. "Did you get the mower you wanted?"

"She got a Murray. Jewed old Colvard down fifty dollars. I got her a senior discount on top of that. Colvard was fit to be tied."

Opal laughed. "Sounds like she knows what she's doing."

He settled in for his sandwich, the sound of the mower rising and falling as Danny ran up and down the hill. Opal told him about Renata planting the orange flowers. He told her about Danny showing him the Quad at Duke.

Opal glanced out the window as the mower circled the hilltop. "She's going mighty fast."

He cocked an ear, the sound of the mower fading, then suddenly growing loud. He got up and went to the window. "She's tipped it over. You stay here in case we need to call someone."

"Oh, Lord."

He walked fast to the bottom of the hill, fear mounting as he saw the mower upside down and Danny sprawled on her back. Thanks to his disconnecting the cut-off switch, the engine was still running, the mower blades slicing the air. He reached under the steering wheel and cut the engine off.

Danny struggled to her feet.

"You alright?"

She rubbed her arm. "I think I jammed my shoulder."

"I told you to run it in third."

"You were right. I thought I could go faster.

Renata came running down the drive. "Oh, my God, are you hurt?"

"I'm alright."

"What happened?"

"I rounded the corner too fast."

The engine ticked as the heat bled off. Gasoline vapors filled the air. Renata glared at Hurley. "You two need to put those thing-a-ma-jigs back on. It's not safe."

She turned on her heel and went back up the drive.

He looked at Danny. "You ready to turn this back over."

They crouched down together and pushed the mower upright, the wheels landing with a loud bang.

Chapter 17

By September, the fall gardens were coming in. Hurley, Renata, and Danny climbed into the tractor and wagon and headed out to the field. The land was hard from the lack of rain, dogwoods sagging in the forest. Only the tended gardens looked lush.

Hurley took the spray can from the wagon and set about dousing the weeds on his side of the garden. Renata and Danny got down on all fours, pulling the weeds that grew between the newspaper.

Passing down the opposite row, he waved his nozzle at Renata. "You sure you don't want some of this?"

"Get that thing away from me."

"Makes things easy."

He worked his way down the rows of beets and okra, then traded the spray can for a watering can. He poured some water on the ground around the okra and paused to look at the sky.

"Light's going early."

Renata looked up. "I love this time of year. The sky is so clear."

"Football starts next week."

Danny groaned. “Football. Another 0 and 14 season for Duke.”

“I don’t pay Duke no mind.”

“How can you live in Durham and not root for the home team?” Renata said.

“Nobody I know went to Duke. Students are all from out of town. Soon as they finish, they up and leave.”

“We’re not going anywhere.”

“That’s what they all say.”

Renata and Danny exchanged looks.

“We have something to tell you,” Renata said. “We’re going to have a commitment ceremony in October.”

“Commitment?”

“It’s like getting married,” Danny said. “We’d do that if the law allowed it. This is the closest thing.”

He stared. “Have you told your folks?”

“I have,” Renata said.

“Wha’d they say?”

“At this point, they’re kind of like, ‘whatever.’”

He turned to Danny. “How about your folks?”

“They don’t want to hear about it,” she said.

He nodded. “It’s kind of different.”

“We want to ask a favor,” Renata said. “We want to have the ceremony out here.”

“In the field?”

“Yes. It’s so beautiful.”

He shook his head. “Time was people couldn’t wait to get out of the fields.”

Danny walked into the grass a short distance from the garden. “We’re hoping you could bush hog a circle where people could sit. We’ll bring out chairs for the older folks.”

"You and Opal are both invited, of course," Renata said. "I'm hoping she could make us one of her famous carrot cakes."

He cocked his head. "I'm gonna have to talk to her about that."

"Hey, I understand," Danny said. "Just let us know how she feels."

* * *

Back in the kitchen, he broke the news to Opal. She stopped in the midst of making a pie crust. "They what?"

"They want to get committed. It's like being married, but you don't have a license."

She sprinkled flour on the pastry cloth and rolled out the dough. "What do their parents say?"

"Renata said hers are going along. Danny's don't like it."

Opal shook her head. "I don't know why people think they can do such things."

"It's not being married," he said. "That ain't allowed."

"Maybe we ought to ask Reverend Shively."

He waved his hand. "You know what he'd say."

He sat at the table, pulled a toothpick from the container. "I can tell them go ahead and use the field, but we can't be a part."

Opal worked the dough. "That's how we treated Patsy."

He startled at the mention of their daughter. Why would she bring Patsy up? He pushed the toothpick between his teeth.

"Renata asked if you could bake them a cake," he said.

"A cake?"

"What she said."

"I swear." She dusted her hands on her apron and sat down at the table. "Did she say what kind?"

Chapter 18

Opal rang the doorbell and waited with her cake pan and bag of pecans. Renata welcomed her in. "You haven't been inside since Buddy and Leanne left, have you?"

"This is the first time."

Opal stepped through the great room into the kitchen.

"It's so kind of you to help with the cake," Renata said. "I can't wait to see your recipe."

"Hurley told me y'all were trying to save money." She glanced around the room. They'd set that funny looking couch against the wall facing the sliding glass door. Above the fireplace, there was a watercolor painting of an Indian woman on horseback.

"We've changed a few things," Renata said. "Danny put that track light in to brighten up the corner."

She switched on the light and the painting came to life. It was kind of strange. In the corner where her and Hurley's used to be were two family photographs.

"Are these your parents?" Opal asked. "Your mother's pretty. You got her eyebrows."

She studied the magnets on the refrigerator. One looked like it came from a comic book. A handsome man in a suit was trying to kiss a woman. "Sorry, dahling," the woman said. "I just can't love a Republican." Opal guessed that meant Danny and Renata were Democrats.

Renata pulled two sheet cake pans out from under the oven. "These two are the same size as yours," she said. "Do you think three will be enough for sixty people?"

"I get eighteen pieces out of mine," Opal said. "Three gives you fifty-four. Usually, not everyone eats cake."

Opal took the well-worn piece of paper out of her dress pocket and unfolded it on the counter. "Here's that recipe. I like to use pecans in the icing. We've got so many of them off the tree."

"Oh, you put cinnamon in yours."

"Just a little."

Opal studied Renata's tall, slender figure. "Do you have a dress to wear?"

"Yes, I'm wearing my mother's old wedding dress! I just got it back from the seamstress. Come look at it before we get our hands dirty."

Renata led the way down the hall to the master bedroom. It had a queen bed now, taking up just about the whole space. Candles lined the headboard, some of them burned down to nubs.

Renata went to the closet and held the dress out for Opal to see. It was an ivory colored satin with an embroidered bodice.

"That's pretty. Does it fit you good?"

"Perfect. I had the hem taken up so it wouldn't drag in the grass."

Above the closet, a picture mirror hung at a downward angle. "That's an odd place for a mirror," Opal said.

She waited for an explanation, but Renata just smiled.

Back in the kitchen, Renata fished through the cabinets.

"What size bowl do you want?" she asked.

"What, now?"

Renata repeated the question.

"Medium will be alright."

Opal tried to concentrate, but her mind kept drifting back to that mirror. Why was it up there? It seemed, as she thought about it, to be aimed at the bed.

"I generally beat everything by hand," Renata said, "But as much as we have to do, I'm going to use a mixer."

The whir of the mixer filled the kitchen. "So those pecans come from your tree?" Renata said. "I love the idea of using stuff from the farm."

Opal chopped pecans and mixed them into the icing.

"What was your wedding like?" Renata asked.

"It was just a regular church wedding. We got married kind of young. My mother planned the whole thing."

"Did you have a honeymoon?"

"We went to Myrtle Beach. It was real nice. We even rode the roller coaster."

"No way. Hurley and you on a roller coaster?"

Opal laughed. "It was the last time, believe you me."

Renata shut off the mixer and poured the cake mixture into the first pan. "How long were you married before you had Patsy?"

"She was born the year we were married. Hurley and I didn't hardly get to know each other as a couple. I kind of regret that."

Renata nodded. "I've heard my parents say the same thing."

"How long have you and Danny been together?"

"Three years. I was married before I met her."

"To a man?"

"Yes. For five years. We're still friends."

Opal was thoroughly confused. How could a woman like men and then like women? Had Renata always been a lesbian and just changed at some point? Or did she still like men and women both?

Chapter 19

Hurley was mowing the front lawn, rounding the corner by the road, when a fancy blue sports car turned in the drive. For a moment, they ran side-by-side, the man behind the wheel peering at him through mirrored sunglasses. The car sped on, leaving a trail of dust.

At the top of the hill, a dark-haired couple got out of the car. He cut short his path, angling across the lawn to the barn. He parked the mower and went into the house.

"Did you see them people next door?" he said to Opal.

She looked up from writing her grocery list. "I expect they might be Renata's parents. They favor the picture in the house."

"The man gave me a look coming up the drive."

"I can imagine."

He poured himself a glass of ice tea and sat at the table. "How many did they say is coming tomorrow?"

"Sixty."

"I told Danny they could park behind the house. I'm gonna make a sign."

Opal furrowed her brow. "Do you want me to do the lettering?"

"Why would I need help with that?"

Without waiting for an answer, he headed for the barn. Opal do the lettering? How stupid did she think he was? He found a piece of scrap plywood tucked in the corner and carried it to the toolshed. He took a pencil from the toolbox and, setting the plywood on the workbench, drew an outline of an arrow and the word "PARKING."

It took a few redraws to get all the letters to fit. He opened a can of black paint, filled in the arrow and thickened the letters. He nailed the sign to a tomato stake, and carried it over to the drive.

Laughter rose as he approached the car shed. Everybody was relaxing on the deck, having a drink. He picked a spot near the corner of the drive and hammered on the stake. The ground was rock-hard. He went back to the tool shed and grabbed a sledge hammer and a two-foot length of galvanized pipe. He banged a hole with the pipe, then tapped the sign in nice and easy.

Renata called out, "Hurley, come over and meet my parents."

He waved, pointed at his tools.

"Come on. Put your sledge hammer down."

As Hurley climbed the steps, Renata's father stood and offered his hand. "I'm Franco. This is my wife, Maria."

The lady held up an arm clinking with gold bracelets. "Renata has told us all about you."

He grinned. "Wha'd she say?"

"She says you're wonderful!"

He asked where they'd driven up from.

"Miami," Franco said. "We took a couple of days."

"I've been to Florida. Disney World."

"That's about two hours north," Maria said.

"I like that Disney World."

Franco held up his glass. "Sit down and have a drink with us."

He eyed the clear booze in the glasses, gin or maybe vodka. He could taste that gin as if it was yesterday. "Thank you. I'll just sit for a spell."

"Renata tells me you've been a big help in getting ready for the wedding," Maria said.

"I ain't done much."

She pointed her drink across the drive. "I love your sign with the backwards 'N'."

Renata frowned. "Mom."

He turned and realized what he'd done. Blood rushed to his head.

Danny jumped in. "Hurley's helping us plant a garden," she said. "Back through those woods."

Maria jiggled the ice in her empty glass. Her voice was slurred. "We had a nice garden, didn't we, Renata? Then, Franco sold the lot."

Franco scowled. "How else was I supposed to pay the bills?" He turned to Hurley. "Castro drove us out of Cuba in '60. He took everything."

"That right?"

"Of course, Renata would like us to make friends with the Communists. 'Normalization.' Your Senator Helms has been very good about stopping that nonsense."

"Jesse's a good man."

Danny rolled her eyes. "Great. Jesse Helms."

Hurley felt his blood rise. Franco, too, was scowling. He didn't care for Danny.

Maria broke into Spanish, arguing with Franco over what he'd said. This would be a good time to leave. He stood and thanked them for the hospitality. Maria broke off arguing, raised her glass, and offered a slow and sloppy toast. "Here's to you, Hurley."

* * *

The helpers began arriving at noon, unloading folding tables and chairs from a van and setting them up in the back yard. Most looked like women, but there were a couple of men, included the colored boy who helped with the move. Hurley watched to see how they interacted, sensed that some of them women willfully ignored the men. He wondered how he and Opal would be treated. If they were ignored, they'd just come back inside after the ceremony.

Opal came out of the bedroom wearing a church dress and heels. "Do you think this looks alright?"

He glanced at her, then back out the window. "Looks fine."

"Are you going to wear your jacket and tie?"

"I'll wear a tie. I ain't putting on a jacket to stand in a field."

"I bet the parents will have on jackets."

Guests began to arrive, parking as the sign directed in his back yard. People walked past the kitchen window wearing all kinds of clothes—women in granny boots and dresses like in the Westerns, men with Hawaiian shirts and straw fedoras.

"Here comes Magnum P.I.," he said.

"You need to get dressed," Opal said. "It's already two o'clock. The ceremony starts at three."

He showered and put on a white short-sleeved shirt and a striped tie. He combed his hair and stepped with Opal into the October sunshine.

Opal smiled. "They got a pretty day. Must be 70."

"First week in October is always nice."

He took Opal's arm and fell in line behind the guests headed out the tractor path. In her heels, Opal wobbled on the hard earth. He thought this whole enterprise foolish. Then, they arrived at the field. The circle he had bush-hogged in the grass was filled with color—joyful figures in all manner of dress. The poplars and maples bordering the field glowed yellow and orange. White clouds sailed across a deep blue sky.

"My Lord," Opal said. "It looks like a country fair."

They walked into the field and stood at the edge of the circle. A woman offered them chairs. Except for Franco and Maria seated up front, they were the only older people.

"I guess Danny's parents decided not to come," Opal said.

He shook his head. "That's a shame." He was hoping to meet these fellow Southerners with the lesbian daughter. Maybe, like he and Opal, they weren't so brave.

Danny and Renata sat on a bench facing the audience, Renata in her mother's old-timey wedding dress, Danny a gray suit. Between them sat a lady with a black robe and a multi-colored stole.

"That must be the preacher," he said.

Opal frowned. "I didn't think women were allowed."

A woman with a violin sat in a chair to one side. At a nod from the preacher, she started to play. It was a familiar song—"Jesu, Joy of Man's Desiring." Midway through the song, a red-tailed hawk appeared from the edge of the treeline and circled overhead.

He nudged Opal. "Looky there!"

"Hush, now," she said.

When the song ended, the preacher stood and welcomed everybody to the ceremony. She started to read from the Bible. "When I was a child, I spoke like a child, I thought like a child, I reasoned like a child..."

That must mean she was a Christian. But how could she ignore the Bible's teaching against women laying with women?

"For now, we see only a reflection as in a mirror; then we shall see face to face. Now, I know in part, then I shall know fully, even as I am fully known."

He never knew what to make of that passage. What did it mean if the more fully you knew some people, the less you believed what Scripture said about them?

The preacher closed her book and asked Danny and Renata to stand. They reached into their pockets and produced a pair of rings. The preacher held them aloft.

"These rings are a symbol of your love for each other," she said. "As circles, they have no end, but like love, they do have a beginning..."

The minister talked about taking the ore from the earth and making it into metal "through intense heat". She compared that to forging a bond of love. He thought about the things these women had gone through—rejection by family and friends, people throwing eggs at them...

"I now pronounce you partners for life."

Danny and Renata kissed. And they kissed. Opal blanched. Renata's father scowled. When the two of them finally quit, the guests clapped and cheered. The preacher declared the ceremony at an end.

As he walked the path home, he waited for Opal to speak. "What did you think?" he asked.

"It was kind of strange," she said. "The kissing and all. I don't agree with that."

He ventured a positive note. "I guess they'll be sticking around."

Back in the yard, women were bringing out food and setting it on the tables. A string band unpacked their instruments on the deck.

He grinned. "Looks like we're going to have a hoe down."

Opal tugged on his arm. "Come on and help me with the cake. I can't carry all three trays."

In the kitchen, she took the Saran Wrap off of the carrot cake. She'd put it on cookie sheets covered with aluminum foil. He picked up two and held the door for Opal.

By the time they returned to Danny and Renata's, the yard was packed with women, talking loud and exchanging hugs. He maneuvered his way to the food table and set the cake next to the punch. Out of nowhere, a colored boy came up to greet him.

"My name's Omar," he said. "I saw you the day I helped Danny and Renata move in."

Hurley shook his hand.

"I was admiring your place. I love all these old buildings."

"You like them?"

"I grew up on a farm in Oxford. We had the same set up."

"Are you still farming?" He knew from the smoothness of the boy's hand that this could not be true. But it was all he could think to say.

"I'm in a dance troupe."

"Dancing? What kind of dancing?"

"Modern dance. Have you ever heard of Alvin Ailey?"

"Ailey?"

"We perform all over the country. You ought to come and see us. We perform at Duke a couple of times a year."

Omar offered his hand again. Hurley watched him leave. Now, there was a nice fellow. Awfully brave to come right up to an old white man.

Opal arrived with the rest of the cake. He started to tell her about Omar, but she cut him off.

"I don't know if we should cut the cake or not," she said.

"That's normally something the couple does. I have no idea about this crowd."

Renata's parents appeared.

"How did you two enjoy the ceremony?" Maria said.

"It was right was nice," Opal said.

"Wasn't it just lovely out there? I would have preferred it had been in a church, but Renata had one of those and we saw how that worked out."

"Children don't always do the way you'd like."

Maria laughed. "That's the truth. I've learned to just keep smiling."

Franco remained silent. He surveyed the food. "I'm ready to eat. Won't you join us?"

Hurley scanned the offerings brought by the guests. There were little white squares covered with something that looked like barbecue sauce. He scooped one onto his plate where it giggled like Jello. The green salad had some kind of flowers on top. Marigolds! Was he supposed to eat those? He passed on the salad and helped himself to cheese puffs, lasagna, and a cup of punch.

The two couples stood off to the side, watching the others while they ate. Franco went into the house and came out with two bottles of Vodka. He set them on the table and mixed himself and Maria drinks. The band struck up a tune and some of the women started to clog.

"I hope they cut that cake pretty soon," Opal said. "I'm ready to head back to the house."

"We've only been here an hour," Hurley said.

"Standing around hurts my back."

The sun went down, the blue sky grew pale and a chill set in. A sip of that Vodka would sure warm things up. Someone lit the tiki torches and the yard seemed transformed into an exotic jungle. The band played a fast banjo song and the dancers went wild.

Opal looked again at the food table. "I guess no one's interested in my cake. Let's go on back."

"I'm gonna stay awhile," he said.

"Come on, now. Let them have their fun."

"I ain't stopping them."

Opal shook her head and retreated across the drive. When he saw the shade come down over the kitchen window, Hurley wandered back to the food table, helped himself to another plate of lasagna. He glanced again at the window. The lights were out. He sidled up to the bottle, poured himself a fingerful, and threw it down. You could barely taste a good Vodka, but the feeling of joy went straight to his head. Shadows flickered on the trees. Voices grew loud. He poured himself another.

Suddenly, Renata was standing in front of him. She looked like a maiden from a picture book, a strand of dark hair hanging across her cheek, eyes huge in the wavering light.

"I caught you, Hurley."

"Don't tell Opal."

"You know I won't."

The band struck up a waltz.

"Come dance with me," she said.

"Nah, I ain't much for dancing."

"I'll show you."

She led him in front of the band, put one of his hands against the small of her back and held the other against her palm. She smelled like honeysuckle, felt firm as a boy. She called out the steps. "One, two, three; one, two, three..."

Someone yelled from the crowd. "Go Hurley!"

He felt himself growing younger, his steps quick and light. The trees became a blur. His head spun. Banjo music, smiling faces, tumbling, tumbling back in time. He clung to Renata for all he was worth.

Chapter 20

When Buddy and Patsy were young, Hurley used to spend at least one Saturday each summer at the Fish Camp in Rougemont. Opal wasn't wild about his going there. She knew about the drinking. But she also knew it was his one chance to get away and be with other men.

Saturday morning, he sat down with the family for a pancake breakfast. Buddy laid a gangly arm across the table to get the maple syrup.

"Don't reach," Patsy said.

Patsy was coming on a young woman. She had a woman's figure, but no boyfriends yet. Not many friends at all. But she seemed to care enough about her younger brother to try and rid him of bad table manners.

"Please pass the syrup," Buddy said.

"Hurley, why don't you take Buddy with you today?" Opal said. "He'd love to do some fishing."

"He's not old enough to stay out."

"Bring him back after dinner. You don't need to stay out all night."

"He's got chores to do."

A little smile crossed Patsy's face. "I know why you won't take Buddy with you."

He glared at Patsy. She might know and then again she might not. He pushed back his chair and reached for his cap. "I'll be back after dark."

Opal called after him. "We've got church tomorrow."

North of town the country opened up to horse pastures and low hills. People from away always talked about how green North Carolina was. He didn't understand what they meant. What other color would the land be? There were different *shades* of green—the dark green of the pines, the blue-green of rye grass, the yellow-green of tobacco. Maybe North Carolina had more of those.

Just past the turn off for Bahama, he pulled into Tommy's Bait Shop. He stepped through the door to the smell of warm dirt and the chirping of crickets. Tommy sat in his wheelchair behind the cash register, a big man with camouflage pants and a hostile stare leaning against the counter.

"Everybody doing alright?" Hurley asked.

"Can't complain," Tommy said.

"I'll take me a carton of nightcrawlers."

Tommy rolled his wheelchair to the worm bin. "Bream are hitting on crickets. You want some of those, too?"

He shook his head. "I'm fishing for bass."

The big man kept staring. Some of these country boys were simple, some downright mean.

Tommy put the carton of worms on the counter. "You headed out to the club?"

"That's right."

The big man spoke. "You know Rick Hill?"

He shook his head.

"Best fisherman around here. Bass, bream, you name it. He'll catch 'em all."

"That right?"

He took his carton of worms and headed out the door, feeling the man's eyes on him all the way. He was glad to get back on the road, gladder still to see the sign on the tree "Rougemont Fish Club—Members Only."

The dirt drive ran through the woods, opening onto a clearing with a one-room cabin, a brick barbecue grill and two picnic tables. Enis Mangum and Web Fuller were already there. He parked his truck next to Enis' and got out his gear.

The pond lay still in the afternoon light, reflecting the surrounding pines. Enis fished from the dock, Web at the far end by the dam.

He called to Enis. "Catching anything?"

"Not to speak of."

"How 'bout Web?"

"He caught one about an hour ago. Been jerking off ever since."

He walked part way around the pond to where Enis and he could carry on a conversation. He plucked a worm from his carton and ran a hook through the crop. Buddy would have wanted to know if the worm was feeling pain. He would have told him no, though the critter's writhing said otherwise. The point was if you wanted to catch fish, you couldn't allow that kind of thinking.

He cast out and set the drag. "Anyone else coming?"

"Owen said he'd be by. Riley'll be out with his shine."

That was the word he wanted to hear. Just the thought of it warmed his throat. This was another reason he couldn't bring Buddy. It was one or the other.

A red-and-white dot in green water, his bobber began to wobble. He set the hook. The fish made a short, zig-zagging run, then gave up. He lifted it in the air, a big head like a bass and a flat body like a panfish. He frowned. "Looks like a warmouth."

"Sure does," Enis said. "I don't know how they get in here, but we don't want 'em."

"They don't fight for shit." He tossed the fish behind him in the grass and cast out again.

"You get your tobacco in?" Enis said.

He nodded. "Got some niggers to help me."

"There's some good ones out there."

A light breeze sent his bobber drifting across the surface. He was glad not to have to farm full time any more. He hated working all day in the hot sun, hated the sticky feel of the tobacco leaves. A farmer never stopped worrying, never stopped working. At American Tobacco, you punched out at the end of the day and went home without a care. You got paid sick days and holidays. There was never a bad year. People always smoked.

The bobber went down fast. He pulled back, felt the heft of a big fish. The line moved slowly sideways, then gathered speed as the bass shot into the air.

"Woo hoo!" he shouted.

The bass landed with a splash and made a run for deep water, stripping line from the reel. He held firm. "Where you think you're goin', boy?"

The bass came into view, bulldogging along with slow sweeps of his tail. One more run and it was through. He lifted the fish by the lower jaw and held it in the air.

"That's a five pounder, at least," Enis said. "Web, you see this?"

Hurley turned the fish side to side, admiring its bulk. There was no finer feeling than catching a big bass in front of your friends. He filled his bucket with pond water and lowered the fish inside.

As the sun went down in the pines, the water took on a silky sheen. He took a bag of Red Man out of his shirt and filled his cheek. Late season crickets chirped in the grass. Single songs you could pick out, not the din of the bait shop.

A black pick-up pulled into the parking area.

"Here's Riley," Enis said. "Quittin' time for me."

Hurley reeled in. "I'm ready for a taste."

He picked up his bucket, heavy now with the water and the prize, and started for the picnic area. Riley nodded as he came up the bank. "Hear you caught a big one."

He lifted his bucket. "Barely fits."

"That's what my wife says."

Riley took a bag of charcoal from his truck and emptied it on the grill. "Somebody light that for me."

Enis stepped forward and struck a match while Riley went to the truck. He came back with a cooler, took out a package of hot dogs and a can of beans.

Hurley eyed the cooler. "Is that all you got?"

"What else you want?" Riley said.

Enis and Hurley exchanged glances.

"Oh, you mean this," Riley said, lifting the jar of clear moonshine.

He smiled. "That's what I'm talking about."

Web unlocked the cabin. "Bring that shine in here," he said. "Getting buggy outside."

As he entered the lamp-lit warmth of the cabin, he smelled mildew, suspected the mattresses on the iron bunk beds. Someone had put sunglasses on the mounted deer head. Last year's outdoor magazines still lay on the table.

He settled into a canvas-cushioned chair and unscrewed the jar. The 100 proof alcohol sent a jolt through his body. "Whoo boy, that'll clean the crust off your pecker."

He passed the jar to Enis. "Hey, Web, did you hear what Opal said to Hurley when he showed her his hard on?"

"Wha'd she say?"

"Now that you've got the wrinkles out, it'd be a good time to wash it."

Hurley laughed with the others. Opal might have actually liked that joke.

"I got one," he said, "How do you make a hot dog stand?"

"Suck it off," Web said.

"No. Take away his chair."

The men groaned. He was not great with jokes. Mostly he liked for the other men to tell them.

"How do you fuck a fat woman?" Web asked. "Roll her in dough and look for a wet spot."

As the men got drunker, the jokes were getting cruder. Another reason not to bring Buddy out here.

Riley came in with the hot dogs. "Make sure these go down the right hole," he said. "I don't want to have to send anybody home." Web found some paper plates and plastic forks in one of the cabinets. Hurley wolfed his hotdogs down and chased them with sips of shine.

Darkness fell. The jokes went around with the hooch. At some point, the cabin started to spin. Hurley remembered trying to get up to take a pee and sinking back into his chair.

When he woke, only Enis was left, passed out on one of the bunk beds. A gray-white sky shone through the window. He checked his watch—8 am—dragged himself to his feet and stumbled out the door. The bass was dead, bent stiff in the curve of the bucket. He set it and his fishing gear in the back of the truck, and climbed into the driver's seat. His head throbbed. How did he let this happen again?

Opal was sitting in the kitchen with the children, dressed and ready for church.

"Get changed," she said. "We'll wait."

He went into the bedroom and put on his Sunday clothes, washed his hands to get the fish smell off.

As they were all going out to the car, Patsy turned and smiled, a forgiveness he didn't deserve.

Chapter 21

She was the apple of his eye. Not the prettiest girl, nor the most talkative, but Patsy had common sense. She never had to be reminded to do her homework, always did her chores well. She liked hanging out with Hurley when he was working on mechanical things, less so with Opal and her domestic chores.

On a Friday evening in June, during Patsy's senior year in high school, he went out to the barn to adjust the cultivator on the tractor. The weeds had set in between the rows of the young tobacco plants in the back field. With a small adjustment, the cultivator could be used to root out the weeds and throw some extra dirt around the growing plants.

Parked under the barn's shed roof with the low sun coming in, the faded red Farmall tractor fairly glowed. The design hadn't changed much since the 1930s. He took comfort in that, knowing that someone had made something just right. He set a stool close to the engine, breathed in the faint smell the motor oil, pleasing as perfume on a woman.

"Do you need help, Pa?"

Patsy stood in the driveway wearing her jeans and T-shirt. He nodded at the cultivator. "You can hold this up while I loosen the nut."

She squatted down beside him and grabbed one of the cultivator's talon-shaped tines. He put a wrench to the nut that held the adjustment pin and pulled hard.

"I ought to have sprayed a little oil on these threads so they don't get rusted up."

The nut came loose and he tapped the pin upward with a hammer.

"Now, turn those in."

Patsy angled the tines inward. "Like this?"

"Just a tad more." He tightened the nut and moved to the other side.

"It's Friday," he said. "How come you aren't out with your friends?"

"What friends?"

He glanced at her. "You don't have any friends?"

"One. Jane Parsons."

"Aren't any boys interested in you?"

"No. And I don't care about boys."

He yanked on the wrench. "People start talking if you don't show any interest in boys."

Patsy fell silent.

"Have you talked to your mother about this?" he asked.

"She said why don't I try growing my hair longer."

"It might help."

"Pa. It won't help."

He didn't want to think of what she was implying. People were not kind to a woman who lived by herself. Worse if she lived with another woman. He couldn't even think of one who did that.

"Pass me that hammer."

Chapter 22

Mid-November, the leaves started coming down, the red maples and poplars first, then the dogwoods, and, finally, the oaks. Hurley watched the big leaves spiral to the ground, spotting the lawn he'd just raked. Danny and Renata seemed content to let the leaves cover their lawn. Maybe they were waiting until everything was down before raking, but if it rained, the leaves would be so heavy you could hardly move them. They didn't seem to care that their leaves made extra work for him. Every time the wind gusted from the west, their leaves blew into his yard. Did they think he was going to rake everything for them?

Saturday morning, a warm front came through sending the temperature up to 65 degrees. He was sitting on the porch chewing tobacco when Danny came out the front door, looking as if she'd just woken up.

He called to her, "Leaves are coming down thick today."

She stared at the treetops. "Yeah. Still a bunch of them up there."

"I'd get to raking if I was you. Come a big rain, you'll have a mess."

Danny crossed the drive. He nodded toward a chair. "Come on and sit a spell."

Across the valley, the hillside had turned from yellow to bronze. "This sure is a nice view from here," Danny said.

Hurley pointed toward the ranch house. "I told Buddy he ought to build him a front porch, but he wanted the deck in back."

She studied the house. "I don't think there's enough slope on our roof to build a porch."

Danny was probably right. He was surprised that she knew enough about construction to make that conclusion. Her daddy must have taught her some things.

"How's Duke?"

"Pretty well. We're getting close to wrapping up the semester."

"You still teaching religion?"

"Yep. We spent last week talking about the Axial Age."

"Is that when they come up with the wheel?"

Danny laughed. "It's Axial, not axle. It was a time when a lot of the major religions were formed. There's some interesting theories about why this happened when there was essentially no communication between the cultures. Some people think there was a coevolution of human thought."

"You believe in evolution?"

"Yes, but this is something else. It means that for some unknown reason, people who had no connection to each other developed similar ways of looking at the world."

"Maybe God spoke to 'em."

"But why would the religions be different?"

"Maybe some of 'em didn't hear right."

This time, Danny laughed with him. He felt good about that, spat into his can. "Supposed to get cold again tonight."

"I'd like to have a fire, but we don't have any wood," Danny said. "I guess we could buy some."

"You don't need to buy wood. You got a dead tree practically in your back yard."

He pointed across their rooftop to the leafless oak standing at the edge of the woods.

"I never noticed that," she said.

"I seen it start to die a year ago. When you burn wood, you're always watching the trees. The big limbs start to die, you know you've got some wood coming."

"What do you think it would cost to have it taken down?"

"Cost you a can of gas."

"You'll cut it down for us?"

"I'll cut it, but I ain't splitting it."

"I can probably split it."

He smiled. "You can try."

* * *

After lunch, Hurley put on overalls went to the toolshed to get his chainsaw. He set it on the workbench and checked the tension on the chain. It pulled a good inch away from the bar. He undid the nuts and tightened the screw until the chain snapped tight.

Danny and Renata were both waiting on the back deck.

"Are you gonna help, too?" he said to Renata.

"Of course. What can I do?"

"Make sure the tree don't fall on the house."

He winked at Danny, led the women into the woods. Pushing away the saplings and briars, he reached the oak and touched the saw to the trunk. "I'll make a wedge cut on this side. It should fall between the house and the car shed."

Renata looked uncertainly in the direction of the fall. "Are you sure about that?"

He pointed up at a rotten limb. "They call those widow makers. One of 'em breaks off, it'll crack your skull. I'd step you on back to the deck. And give a yell if one of them shakes loose."

He pulled the starter chord and gunned the engine until the smoke ran clear. The women hurried away. He angled the saw from side to side, woodchips spraying from the cut.

When the blade was halfway through the trunk, he pulled it out and angled a second cut down above the first. The cuts met and a watermelon slice of wood popped out. He circled to the backside of the tree and started another cut. As the blade neared the gap, Danny yelled out from the deck, "Thar she goes!"

A cracking split the air as the grain of the oak gave way. The tree swept the sky, whooshed through the saplings, and hit the ground with a jarring thud.

"Woah, man," Danny said. "You landed it perfectly."

Renata hugged her. "Look at all this wood, babe! We are going to have us a fire tonight."

He approached the downed tree. "I'll cut the logs about 22 inches. That's about right for your fireplace. You can stack them between those two pines over by the car shed."

"Where you used to have your woodpile," Danny said.

"The branches are thin enough to burn, but you're gonna have to split this trunk."

He fired up the chainsaw and started cutting the branches. Danny and Renata collected an armload each and carried them into the house. He worked his way down the main trunk and, in an hour's time, the big oak was reduced to pieces.

"You sure you want to split these yourself," he said. "I'd rent me a gas splitter."

"I can split them if you show me how."

He shook his head. "Back of my tool shed there's a maul and a pair of wedges. Bring 'em over and I'll show you."

He turned to Renata. "Let's go inside. I need to show you something about your fireplace."

She opened the sliding glass door. "Take your boots off, please. This shag rug is a dirt magnet."

"I wouldn't have shag in my house, but Leanne had insisted on it."

He knelt down in front of the fireplace, took a poker from the rack and shoved it up the chimney. "The handle on this damper is broken. If you want a fire, you need to push it open."

Renata nodded. "I'll tell Danny."

He wiped his hands on his trousers and looked around the room. The Indian painting Opal had talked about hung on the wall. On the coffee table was a small pottery vase holding some kind of sticks.

"What's this?"

"Incense," she said. "Here, smell."

She held a stick to his nose.

"You burn it and it opens up your senses. You and Opal ought to try it sometime." She gave him a flirtatious smile.

Something inside him stirred. Never in his life had he heard a woman say such a thing.

Out on the lawn, Danny arrived with the maul and wedges. Hurley propped a log on end and pointed to the cracks radiating from the center. "You need to find the biggest crack. That's where it likes to split."

He centered the maul on the log and took a swing. The blade wedged in the wood. He pried it out and handed the maul to Danny. "Put one of those wedges in and give it a try."

She tapped the wedge into the crack and took a swing. The maul glanced off the wedge and toppled the log. She grabbed her lower back.

"Hurts when you miss, don't it?" he said.

Danny set the log back on end. "I can do it."

She swung again, hitting the wedge dead center. The log split half way, long fibers holding it together.

"Give it one more," he said. "Not too hard."

Another swing and the two halves fell to the ground. He nodded, picked up the chainsaw. "I'm going on back to the house. You need anything, come knock."

* * *

With the sun gone down in the trees, Hurley settled into his recliner and turned on the football game. Opal sat on the couch knitting a sweater for L. Dog, a bag of purple yarn at her feet. The clink of the splitting maul rang across the hill.

"Sounds like she's getting it pretty well," Opal said.

"She learns quick. She's strong."

"I'm surprised you didn't do the whole thing for her."

The truth was his back hurt just from the one swing he took with the maul. He never used to feel that way. It occurred to him that in a few short years, there would be a lot of things he wouldn't be able to do around the farm. Who would help him with things like cutting wood, cleaning out the gutters? Buddy only came by occasionally. He couldn't ask the neighbors to do his work. He closed his eyes to the chatter of the sportscaster and the clink of the maul.

When he woke, the game was over. Opal was in the kitchen basting a chicken. The sky through the window was dark.

"Danny finish up out there?" he asked.

"She quit about a half hour ago," Opal said. "I don't know how far she got. She sure went at it hard."

He went to the window and peered into the darkness. "Supposed to be down to thirty tonight. I'll get the woodstove going."

"Don't do it now. We're about to eat."

Over dinner, Opal brought up the subject of the tree. "You ought to be careful doing things like that for the neighbors. What if that tree landed on the deck?"

He ignored the comment. There were some things you just knew that you couldn't explain to another person. They wouldn't believe you anyway.

After dinner, he went into the living room to watch the sports round-up. Opal knit for awhile then announced she was going to bed. "That bedroom is cold," she said. "I wish you'd turn on the furnace."

He waved her off. With fuel oil at a dollar a gallon, he didn't like running the furnace. He would use the wood stove as long as he could.

The show finished, he put on his jacket and hat and stepped outside. A full moon had come up casting the shadows of trees across the yard. The smell of wood smoke drifted from Danny and Renata's chimney. Already, they had a fire going.

The cut up tree looked like a giant Tootsie Roll, pieces of the trunk laying end to end in the yard. He crossed the driveway, curious to see how well Danny had done with the splitting. Visible through the neighbor's sliding glass door, orange light from the fireplace flickered on the family room wall. Danny was lying face down on the shag carpet wearing nothing but underpants.

He started to look away when Renata came into the living room wearing a white bathrobe, her hair up in a bun. He stood as still as a heron. She struck a match and lit one of the incense sticks on the table. Kneeling down on Danny's thighs, she unscrewed a bottle of oil and started rubbing her back. He could feel those hands kneading his sore muscles. She straightened up and untied her belt, the terrycloth robe falling to the floor. The sight of Renata's dark-nippled breasts sent blood surging through his veins. His dick began to grow, something that hadn't happened in years. She rolled Danny over and slipped off her drawers, then lowered her head between Danny's thighs, her curvaceous bottom rocking back and forth as she licked open her partner's cunt. Heart-pounding against his overalls, he fled across the drive.

In the bedroom, he shed his clothes, slipped between the sheets, and snuggled up to Opal's warm behind. It took her a moment to notice. "What in tarnation?" She rolled over and saw his smile.

"Hurley Cates!"

Chapter 23

Patsy had just one friend in high school. Jane was a lively girl, smart like Patsy. She came from good people, Grant and Jeanette Parsons who owned the dry cleaners on University and another one in town. Jane came over on occasion. She was friendly with him and Opal, made comments about teachers and funny things that Patsy said. He and Opal listened close, eager to learn what their daughter was like away from home.

Patsy never invited Jane to spend the night. Hurley suspected it was because she was embarrassed by Buddy. But the summer after graduation, when Buddy was away on a church camp trip, Patsy did ask. He and Opal readily agreed.

Over dinner, he questioned Jane about her plans for the future.

"I want to move to New York City to find a job," she said.

He frowned. "What's wrong with Durham?"

"And work for who? American Tobacco?"

That hurt, not just because he and Opal had worked there, but because so many other smart kids were moving out of North Carolina at the first opportunity. Patsy still hadn't made any plans. She'd failed to apply to college and didn't seem in any hurry to find a man.

After dinner, she and Jane said they were going out for a walk. The house was quiet without them, and when the sun went down, he peered out the window, wondering aloud where they had gone.

"They're probably out in the field," Opal said. "I wouldn't worry."

"I'm gonna check the barn."

The big doors were open as always, the tractor parked in the usual place. He walked into the shadows, heard a faint moaning from up in the hay loft. Thinking someone might be hurt, he climbed the ladder against the back wall. He came through the opening and looked over his shoulder. Jane and Patsy lay on the loose hay buck naked.

Patsy yelled. "Pa, get out!"

He ducked down. "You two come down from there."

"Just get out."

"I'm calling Jane's daddy."

"No, you don't!"

He climbed down the ladder and stormed back to the house.

"What happened?" Opal said. "Are they alright?"

"I caught 'em up in the barn messing around with each other."

"What?"

"You know what I mean."

He pulled the phonebook out of the drawer and got Grant on the phone. He explained that Patsy and Jane had been "misbehaving" and that she needed to go home. "You know the kind of thing I'm talking about," he said.

While they waited for Grant to arrive, the girls sat on the porch crying. Every now and then, Patsy would yell through the door, "You are an asshole, Pa! A fucking asshole!"

As soon as Jane departed, she went to her room and slammed the door. Opal tried knocking, but she told her through sobs to leave her alone.

He and Opal lay in bed wondering what to do. "We ought to meet with Reverend Thurber," Opal said. "He knows about these things. I don't have a clue."

He nodded. "We've got to put a stop to it."

The next three days, Patsy refused to talk with them, except to say that she would not meet with Reverend Barber.

"You want to live in this house, you'll meet with him," he said.

Buddy returned from his Scouting trip and sensed that something was wrong. Patsy refused to say anything to him. Opal told him to ask his father.

"They misbehaved," Hurley said. "That's all you need to know."

On Sunday afternoon, Reverend Barber invited the three of him into his office. He listened while Hurley explained what had happened. Patsy stared out the window.

"You understand this is very serious," the Reverend said to Patsy. "You need to resist these feelings and pray that they will go away."

He turned to Hurley and Opal. "She needs to stay away from this friend of hers. That's the most important thing."

Patsy wailed. "She's my only friend."

"She ain't the kind of friend you need," Hurley said.

She stood up and ran out of the office, out the parking lot and down the road. It took Opal's pleading to get her in the car, where she curled into a ball and refused to speak. He could see now that was the beginning of the end.

Chapter 24

Not many friends stopped by the neighbor's house, but those who did were mostly women. Hurley would see them come and go on weekends while he was out working in the yard. But with the onset of winter and early darkness, visitors came and went unnoticed. So he did not know how many times Omar had been there before seeing him on a Saturday afternoon.

"What choo doing here?" Hurley said, when he spied the colored boy stepping out of his car.

Omar crossed the lawn and offered him a hand. "I've just come by for a visit."

"Are you still dancing?"

"Oh, yes. We've got a show in New York next week."

"Are you gonna see the Statue of Liberty?"

Omar laughed. "I'll see her at a distance. I'm not sure I'll get inside."

Twice more over the course of the winter, Omar came by. Both times, Danny was out.

The middle of April, Hurley drove the tractor out to the field, packets of seeds in his coat pocket. The woods around the tractor path glowed electric green, everything coming out at once. The air was fresh, not yet humid. You couldn't help but feel good about being alive.

Danny and Renata were in their half of the garden, kneeling beside a freshly-tilled row. He hadn't seen either of them in a month, other than to wave as they came and went in the driveway. It wasn't until Renata sat back on her heels that he noticed the hard bulge in her belly. Either she had put on weight or she was pregnant. He didn't see how the latter was possible.

"Hey, girl."

"Hey, boy."

He laughed. "I forget you don't like to be called that a'way.

He walked to the farthest row with his stick and made a trench an inch-and-a-half deep. Then he opened his pack of corn seeds and dropped them in every foot. As he approached Renata, he stole another look and caught her glancing back.

"You been behaving yourself?" he said.

She smiled. "Yes. Why would you say that?"

"I was just kidding you."

Each time she dug a hole, Renata reached in a green and yellow bag and sprinkled a handful of powder.

"What you got in the bag?" he asked.

"Organic fertilizer."

"I use a spray."

"I know you do."

"Are you planting tomatoes this year?"

"I thought I'd plant some Marglobes. And cherry tomatoes."

"Them little things?"

"They're great on salads. You ought to try them."

"I like me a big tomato."

At the far end of her row, Danny worked in silence. He had a feeling something was up, and the next time Renata sat up, he pointed with his stick.

"What are you carrying there?" he said.

She stopped working, turned to Danny. "Shall we tell him?"

Danny dusted off her hands. "We're going to have a baby."

He stood dumbfounded.

"We didn't want to tell anyone until we knew it was going to happen," Renata said.

He looked back and forth at the women. "Who's the daddy?"

Renata blushed. "Omar."

A wave of anger rushed over him. A colored man for a father when you could choose anyone. How could they do such a thing?

"Don't worry. It was all planned," Danny said.

"Both of you planned it?"

"That's right."

He shook his head, stared into the distance. He'd tried his best to understand and accept these women. He'd kept his mouth shut when they did things he didn't agree with. But this was too much.

"You know what color baby that's going to be?" he asked.

"I hope a lovely shade of brown," Renata said.

"You better hope he looks like you, because if he looks like Omar, he's going to have a hard time." Now, the fury was flowing. "A child that looks black is going to be treated bad at school. He'll have a hard time finding a good job. You know what I'm talking about."

"Believe me, it wasn't an easy decision," Danny said. "We're asking a lot of people to accept something they're not used to."

"Most of them ain't going to accept it."

* * *

Opal lowered her knitting. "Omar? The colored boy?"

"What they said."

Her voice rose. "Why would you choose a colored?"

He shook his head. "What I told 'em."

"I don't understand it. Why didn't Renata marry another man if she wanted to have a child?"

"I've got no idea."

"You're out there all the time with them. You should know something."

"I didn't even know she was pregnant until today. How am I going to know about the Daddy?"

She looked out the window. "To think I baked them a cake."

The two of them were silent over dinner. He knew Opal felt he was somehow to blame for this. Always going across the drive to see if there was something he could help them with. Flirting with Renata like he was 20-years old.

"I think we need to talk with Reverend Shively about this," she said. "I need to know how we're supposed to behave."

* * *

Wednesday morning, she and Hurley met the Reverend in his office. He brought in two metal chairs, offered them both a cup of coffee. Hurley sat rubbing his chin between his fingers like he was trying to work it to a point.

"Tell me what's going on," the Reverend said.

Hurley nodded to Opal. "You tell him."

She explaining how the women, Danny and Renata, had come to move next door, how they "seemed like nice enough people" at first. She described how Hurley had always helped Buddy with different chores and could see that these women needed help with things like planting a garden and cutting wood.

"Then in the fall, they decided to get committed," she said. "They said it's like marriage, but not legal. We didn't intend to be a part of it, but they asked and we didn't want to be rude. They had the ceremony out in our back field."

The Reverend listened with furrowed brow as she described how six months later, they announced that Renata was going to bear a child by a colored man.

"The two women agreed to it. We don't know exactly how it was done. We're just not sure how to behave."

Shively shook his head. "This is quite a lot to consider." He got out his Bible and searched for a page. "I appreciate your coming to me for advice. I wish you'd come in sooner. Do you remember the passages I read back when they had that parade?"

They nodded. "We remember."

"So I don't need to remind you of what Romans said about women lying with women?"

Opal shook her head. "No. Huh-uh."

"Now, I'm not going to address the race of this child or the father. The Bible says nothing about the mixing of the races, but I am deeply concerned that these two lesbians seemed to have worked their way into your lives."

Hurley cleared his throat. "One of them might just be half. Renata. She was married before. To a man."

Opal looked at him, annoyed.

"Which only proves the point I was about to make," Shively said. "These women have chosen this lifestyle of sin, it wasn't some accident of birth like they're trying to claim."

He nodded. It made sense about the choosing. But Patsy...

"The devil comes into our lives in many disguises, often pleasant ones," he continued. "But we should not be fooled. Hurley, your wife implies that you are quite taken with these two."

He blanched. "I try to help 'em out."

"That's understandable. But what I am going to advise both of you to do as of now is stop all communication with these women. I realize they live right next door and you're going to run into them from time to time, but you are not to seek them out. You are not to abet their lifestyle in any way. Is that understood?"

Opal put her hand on his. "We understand."

Shively rolled his chair forward and added his hands on top of theirs. "Now, I'm going to ask that we pray for these women." He bowed his head. "Lord, we have discovered a grave sin in our community, a sin being practiced by neighbors of your servants, Hurley and Opal. They are brazen in their sinfulness, joining together as a couple, bearing a child out of wedlock. We pray that you protect Hurley and Opal from their further influence. We pray that, somehow, these women come to recognize the wickedness of their ways, and that they choose to renounce it, so that we may welcome them into your blessed flock. Amen."

Chapter 25

For three months, Hurley ignored them. He waited until they drove off to work before he went down to get the paper. He tended to the back garden in the morning, mowed the lawn in the early afternoon. On weekends, they might pass on the drive as he was mowing. He would offer a wave, same as you would do to a neighbor you passed on the street, but there were no invitations to sit on the porch or carry water out to the back field.

He tried not to even look at them. It hurt too much to see the disappointment on their faces. They were clearly confused about his and Opal's behavior. Even Gus seemed confused, looking back and forth between him and the women if they happened to find themselves in the yard at the same time.

As spring fled before the heat of summer, he began to feel like a prisoner on the hill. He was desperate to tell the neighbors this wasn't his choice, but Opal wouldn't allow it. If she saw either one of them outside, she would call out a warning. "Renata's out on the deck. Danny's getting ready to mow the lawn." She described seeing Renata, heavy with child, load buckets of water into a little Red Flyer wagon to carry out to the field. That earned a note of sympathy from Opal.

"She ought to be careful lifting heavy things," she said. "Her due date's got to be any time."

One Saturday morning, he decided to drive the tractor out to the back field to water the garden. It hadn't rained in three weeks. The forest looked sapped of life, leaves hanging limp from their branches. As he came into the clearing, he saw Renata watering plants, the wagon by her side. Her hard stare filled him with fear.

He stepped down from the tractor. "Hey, girl."

Renata stood and brushed the hair from her face. "He talks."

He managed a weak smile, got one of the buckets from the wagon and approached a row of corn.

"Are you going to tell me why you've been avoiding us?" Renata said.

He poured the water onto the crusted clods, struggled to find the right words.

"It's Omar, isn't it?" she said. "Danny warned me that you white Southerners were all like this. You can't accept a black child in your midst."

He threw her a glance. "It ain't just the child."

"What else?"

He set the bucket down and took a breath. "Me and Opal went to see the preacher, to ask about what you were doing. He didn't speak about the child. Or the Daddy. He said to stay away from y'all."

"To stay away from us? So that what, we don't infect you with our sexual orientation?" Renata's voice trembled with emotion. "I thought you were our friend, and now you're not. Because of what some preacher thinks?"

She burst into tears, covered her face with her hands.

He felt ashamed. "Can I help you with your watering?"

"No, just leave me alone. God." She picked up her bucket and, stumbling over the row, dropped it in the wagon. She headed off down the trail, the air filled with the rattle of the wagon as it bounced over the hard dirt.

* * *

Opal was in the kitchen when he came through the back door.

"I run into Renata out back," he said.

She wiped her hands on the dish towel and sat down with him at the table. "What happened?"

"She wanted to know why we were avoiding her and I told her. She cried like a baby. Probably crying still."

"Oh, my." Opal's face drooped.

"I don't care what the preacher says. You don't treat people this a way."

She shook her head.

"Are you worried about turning lesbian?" he asked.

"No."

"Are you worried about me turning lesbian?"

She chuckled. "I guess not."

"Then why are we treating them so mean? If they're committing a sin with each other, that's their business. They ain't asking us to join in. The Bible says love thy neighbor like thyself. That's my business."

For the first time in months, he felt clear-headed, strong. The words flowed like water bubbling from a spring.

"From here on out, if I feel like talking to them, I'm going to talk. I feel like helping, I'm going to help. And when that baby comes, I'm going over to visit. You can do what you want."

He stuck a toothpick in his mouth and stared out the window, let Opal have her say.

"Well…I just don't know."

Chapter 26

Opal and Hurley waited a week after the baby was born before coming over. She was nervous, not having spoken to either of the women in four months. But they welcomed her as if nothing had happened.

"Have a seat on the couch," Danny said. "Noah's just waking up."

"That's what you're calling him?" Opal said. "That's a nice name."

Renata appeared with Noah and sat next to her on the couch. She pulled back the blanket to reveal cocoa brown face with wavy black hair and barely visible black eyes.

"He's a cute little fella," she said.

Hurley smiled. "Looks like his mama."

"Would you like to hold him?" Renata said to her.

"No, that's alright."

"How about you Hurley?"

He declined as well.

"Go on," Danny said. "He doesn't have cooties."

Opal felt ashamed. "I'll take him just for a minute."

She laid him on her lap and stared into his face. The old maternal feelings rushed in, a feeling of being in the presence of innocence. She put a finger to his forehead and ran it down his nose. A smile flashed across his face.

"Look at him smile," Renata said.

"Buddy always liked that."

Hurley sniffed. "That ain't a real smile."

He reached across Opal and tickled Noah's blanket. "You had him circumcised?"

Danny and Renata exchanged glances. "We've had a difference of opinion on that," Renata said. "But no, we haven't."

"I'd have him circumcised," Hurley said. "You don't want the other boys making fun of him."

Danny nodded. "That's what I said."

"I just don't think it's necessary," Renata said. "It causes a lot of pain."

"He ain't gonna remember."

Renata's eyes flashed. "How do you know?"

He looked at the floor.

"Hurley's of the opinion that pain is good for you," Opal said. "It builds character or some such thing."

"There's all kinds of pain," Hurley said. "Being made fun of is something you don't forget."

She touched Noah's nose. "You'll grow up either way, won't you, Noah? Most of us do."

* * *

The day before Christmas, Opal awoke to find a blanket of snow covering the hill. The lawn, the garden, the driveway, all of it had disappeared. There were no cars on the road. It was as if the Lord had said none of that is important. Look instead on this world of pure white.

At first, Hurley shared in her delight. "Kind of pretty," he said, looking out the front window.

But after walking down the drive and finding no newspaper, he grew restless. "Maybe Buddy could borrow a grader from work," he said at the breakfast table. "Get this driveway cleared."

"You need to relax," she said. "Find something to do inside. I'm going to knit Noah some booties. Do you think they'd like purple?"

"I've got no idea what they'd like."

He got up from the table and stared at their house across the drive. "Women don't come out much now that they've got that baby."

"You shouldn't worry about them. Why don't you make us a fire?"

While Hurley went outside to gather wood, she got out her darning needles and yarn and sat on the living room couch. As she casted on the first row, she considered Hurley's comment about the women. He was sweet on Renata, resented the fact that her attention was going to be focused on someone besides him. And he liked doing chores with Danny. Anything but stay inside.

Hurley came back and stuffed some logs into the stove. He stood for a moment looking through the house. "I'm gonna throw some seed out for the birds," he said.

Half-an-hour later, he was back saying he was hungry. She looked at her watch. "It's only eleven o'clock."

"I'm ready for lunch."

"I'm in the middle of knitting. Fix yourself a sandwich."

He looked like he'd just been delivered a death sentence. "You don't want to eat?"

He wandered back into the kitchen and opened the refrigerator door. Silence. Hurley could take a lawn mower engine apart and put it back together, but when it came to making a sandwich, he didn't know where to start.

She called out, "Do you want ham and cheese?"

"That's what I'm looking for."

"Ham is in the drawer on the left. Cheese is on the right."

He fumbled through the drawers. "There's a couple of cheeses. Which one do I like?"

"Muenster. It's orange on the outside."

"I can't find it."

She put down her knitting and headed into the kitchen. "You're going to starve if I ever get sick."

By mid-afternoon, she had finished Noah's booties. Hurley asked if she wanted to take them over.

"You're sure in a hurry to see those women."

"Tomorrow's Christmas."

They bundled up and went across the drive. Danny answered the door.

"We brought Noah a present." Opal held up the booties.

"Wow, look at those!"

Danny explained that Renata was breastfeeding Noah, but urged them to come in. Opal hesitated. "We can come back another time."

"No, please come in."

They sat on the couch next to Renata. Opal held up the booties.

"Do you think they'll fit him?"

Renata smiled. "Oh, absolutely!"

She glanced at the cocoa-skinned infant suckling on Renata's dark nipple. She wished Renata would cover up. Hurley was looking her way a little too often.

"I see you got your decorations up," she said of the Christmas tree in the corner and the pine boughs and cones laid across the hearth.

"Danny got those branches in the woods," Renata said. "All we need is some mistletoe."

"I'll get you some mistletoe," Hurley said. "Top of that oak right there in your yard." He pointed out the sliding glass doors at a tree at the forest's edge. High up in the naked crown was a branch of mistletoe.

"How are you going to get it down?" Renata said.

"Shoot it."

Opal frowned. "You don't need to be making all that noise on this beautiful day."

"Do you really want it?" Hurley asked.

Renata beamed. "Yes!"

Before Opal could protest any further, he was out the door. "He's been restless as a jaybird," she said.

"My Dad tried shooting down a mistletoe once," Danny said. "It took him about five shots to hit it, then it got caught in the branches."

Hurley appeared in the backyard with his 4-10 shotgun. He broke open the gun and fished in his coat pocket for a shell.

"Come on, Renata," Danny said. "We've got to see this."

"I'll stay inside with Noah," Opal said. "He might not like that noise."

Danny protested. "Oh, he'll be alright."

The two women put on their coats, Renata wrapping Noah in his blanket. Outside, the sun was already down in the trees, the high, whispy clouds tinged with orange. Renata pointed out the snowy landscape to Noah.

"Look at the snow," Renata said. "Isn't it pretty?"

Opal smiled. “It covers up all the sound.”

“Check out the color in those clouds,” Danny said.

She was looking up when the shot popped her ears and rolled across the valley. Noah startled and began to cry. The women clustered around and tried to calm him, while Hurley walked over and picked up his mistletoe, grinning like a fool.

Chapter 27

By late March, the last of the snows had gone, and the temperature climbed into the 60s. Red maples leant the first color to the landscape, the tips of the branches wrapped in tiny saffron robes. If Danny and Renata were serious about wanting to use Marvin's manure to fertilize their garden, now was the time to get it.

He hadn't seen much of the women all winter. Renata would probably be too busy with the baby to come gather manure, but Danny might be game. He hooked the wagon up to the tractor and threw in a dozen pieces of firewood in case Marvin's heat had run out. He pulled up in front of the rancher and knocked on the door.

"Sure I'll come," Danny said. "I need to get out of the house."

"Bring a shovel."

Marvin's house had gone downhill over the past year. A big elm branch lay in the front yard. A gutter dangled from a rotting eave. He parked the tractor and knocked on the door.

Danny looked in a window. "The shades are all pulled."

"He might be asleep."

He knocked again and Marvin emerged wearing a wool cap with the earmuffs down. His eyes lit on Danny.

"That's my neighbor," Hurley said. "She's come to get some more of that manure."

Marvin stepped back. "Come on inside."

"Why are you wearing those earmuffs. It's 65 degrees out."

"I ain't got no heat."

"Again?"

They stepped into the darkened living room.

"You need some light in here," Hurley said.

He opened one of the shades, then walked into the hall to check the thermostat. It was set on 65, but the house was no more than 50. "Your propane must be out. You need to call the man and have him refill your tank. You know where the number is?"

Marvin waved a bony finger. "It's on the refrigerator."

"Meantime, we brought you some firewood."

He instructed Danny to bring some logs in from the wagon and set them in the wood stove.

He walked into the kitchen. "Have you been eating anything?"

"I got some bread, peanut butter and jelly. I don't know what else might be in there."

He checked the refrigerator, sniffed the open carton of milk. "This here's bad. What you got in these cabinets?"

"A few cans of beans and a box of rice."

"You need to eat something more than that. I'll get Opal to fix you some stew."

Danny came in with the firewood. She balled up some newspaper and set it in the stove. When the fire was going strong, she closed the woodstove door and adjusted the air intake.

"How's that feel?" she said to Marvin.

He looked at her. "You say you're staying up at Buddy's?"

"Yes, my partner and I moved in awhile ago."

"Did Buddy die?"

"No, he moved over to the other side of town. We bought his house."

Marvin shook his head. "I don't know what's going on. Nobody tells me."

Out by the wagon, he and Danny gathered up the rest of the wood.

"I can't believe people are living like this," Danny said. "We're ten minutes from the Research Triangle Park."

He frowned. "That's what happens when you get old and your family don't give a shit."

"We ought to call social services."

"Social services?" He shook his head. "That's what neighbors are for. Let's get that manure."

Chapter 28

Hurley pulled into Taylor's Exxon and parked the truck to the side of the pumps. He walked through the open door to find Russell behind the cash register reading the paper.

"What do you say, Hurley?"

He took a Coke out of the cooler and settled into the metal chair. After taking a sip, he examined the bottle.

"Did you change the temperature on that cooler?"

"It's the same as it always is."

"Seems a little warm to me."

Russell tapped the newspaper. "Reagan told the Russians to take down the Berlin Wall. What do you think of that?"

He sniffed. "They ain't gonna take that wall down. Why would they?"

"That Gorbachev's a different man."

He sipped his Coke, looked out the window.

"I saw one of your neighbors in here yesterday," Russell said. "She had a colored baby in the car seat."

"That's Noah."

"Is he adopted?"

He nodded. Better not to get into the details.

"I didn't think that was legal for two women," Russell said. "Where did they get him from, South America?"

"Some place like that."

"I don't know why in the world you'd adopt a colored baby. Must be a shortage of whites."

"Are people talking about it?"

"The women or the baby?"

"Both."

"They want to know when you're going to have an orgy up there."

Hurley grinned. "I already had one."

"So that's why it turned out colored."

* * *

In the morning, he and Opal walked out to the front garden to pick vegetables. Gus ran ahead, chased a ground hog into its hole under the barn. A bluebird lit on the box atop the fencepost, the hatchlings cheeping in a frenzy.

"That's the second brood of the summer," he said. "Usually a snake's got 'em by now."

"Maybe you've shot them all," Opal said.

He shook his head. "You never kill all the snakes."

They set their baskets on the ground and searched out the dark purple sheen of ripe eggplants, the deep green of cucumber, the yellow-orange of summer squash. He was working his way back along the last row when Renata came across the lawn with Noah atop her shoulders. She was barefooted, wearing cut-off jeans and a buttondown shirt. She was starting to get her figure back.

"Hey, there," Renata said. "We've come to see what you're up to."

He missed the days when it was just her. Any baby would be a distraction, but this one especially. Hurley just couldn't get used to that curly black hair.

"Pretty day, isn't it?" Opal said.

"Gosh, you've already got a ton of stuff—cucumber, eggplants, squash..."

"Everything's come in early with the rain," Opal said. "Would you like some for Danny?"

"Absolutely. We haven't had time for a garden this year."

"Let me take these baskets inside and I'll bring one back out for you." She paused to pull on Noah's bare toe.

"He's getting big, isn't he?"

Renata smiled. "Twenty pounds."

Opal headed back to the house leaving him and Renata alone.

"Do you mind if I show Noah your vegetables?" she said.

"Bring him on."

Renata waded into the garden and lifted a cucumber from its stem. "This is a cucumber," she said to Noah. "Hurley grew it. He can grow anything."

Noah looked at him with big eyes. He reached out his hand. "Hur!"

"That's right!" Renata said. "His name is Hurley."

He felt a ping of warmth. "What is that boy, eight months?"

"Nine months next week."

"Buddy didn't talk 'til he was pret' near two."

Renata pursed her lips in sympathy. "Just because someone's late speaking doesn't mean they aren't smart. People have different kinds of intelligence."

That sounded like gobbledy-gook. Still, it made him think. "Buddy never was any good at school work, but he was right quick with machinery," he said. "He was driving that tractor by the time he was thirteen."

"See? They call that spatial intelligence," Renata said.

He imagined Buddy working the controls of a tractor shovel, tipping the bucket, swiveling the arm. It made him feel better about Buddy to think that he had a special skill. And that made him feel warmer toward Renata. He lifted his cap and wiped the sweat from his brow.

"I need to get my scythe and cut that pokeweed behind the barn. Why don't y'all come up? Noah ain't seen that yet."

Hurley led the way through the open double doors. Beams of sunlight slanted down through the gaps in the siding. The dust hung suspended like sand particles in the ocean.

Renata spoke to Noah in breathless tones. "Look at this place. Isn't it beautiful?"

Noah reached out his hand to try and catch the dust.

"And here's a tractor. Wouldn't you love to drive that?"

He led the way to the back of the barn where the scythe leaned against the wall. He brought it into the light and showed Renata the long curving blade.

"That looks dangerous!"

"My daddy passed that on to me. His daddy give it to him."

"I'd have thought you'd have switched to a weed eater."

"This works just as good. You never need to fuss with it."

Out in the yard, he approached the stand of pokeweed. He gripped the twin handles of the bent wooden shaft and started a slow motion swing. The blade sang as it cut through the stems.

"Wow, it's like a big sword," Renata said.

Noah pulled his thumb out of his mouth. "Soar!"

Hurley marched ahead, twisting his hips as he swung the blade. The pokeweed fell before him.

Chapter 29

Danny took her tray from the buffet line and entered the faculty dining room. Profs clustered at the usual places—senior faculty at the big round tables, junior faculty at the tables for four. She crossed the carpeted floor looking for an open chair. Eyes glanced her way, but no invitations followed. Fine, she thought. I'll take a table by myself and see who wants to join me.

One of the black wait staff asked for her drink order.

"I'll have coffee," Danny said. "How are you, Melvin?"

"Fine. How about yourself?"

"Just doing my thing."

"I hear you."

Danny started into her salad, glanced at the people coming from the buffet line. Men and women both, they passed by her table like water around a rock. By the time she was into her chicken and dumplings, she knew she would be dining alone.

She arrived home angry, tossing her jacket on the couch. Renata looked up from feeding Noah in his high chair.

"Are you O.K., honey?"

"No." She went to the refrigerator and took out a bottle of chardonnay.

"What is it?"

"The same old bullshit."

She put a corkscrew to the bottle, poured herself a glass, and sat at the dining room table next to Noah. "Hey, birthday boy. Do you know you're a birthday boy? One year old."

Noah wriggled in his chair, held up a handful of spaghetti. His hair was growing in thick and curly—a little Afro. He had Renata's almond-shaped eyes and her big smile.

"He knows something's up," Renata said. "I told him you are going to give him a big present and he keeps looking around the room."

"Yeah, you're a smart boy," Danny said, pinching his cheek. She finished her wine and poured another glass. Renata regarded her with a frown.

"So what happened exactly?

"I'm not going to get tenure. It doesn't matter what I publish, I'm just not a member of their club."

Renata came over and stroked her hair. Noah pounded on his high chair. "Down!"

Danny did the same on the table. "Yeah, down!"

She took off his bib, lifted him out of the high chair and set him on his feet. "I'm going to bring you a present."

From the closet in the living room, she dragged out the heavy wooden box. She sat beside Noah and tapped the top.

"This was my Dad's when he was young. He didn't have a little boy to give it to, so he gave it to me."

She lifted the top to reveal a set of wooden blocks worn smooth from years of being made into walls, towers, and bridges.

"What do you think of that?"

Noah reached in and began dropping blocks on the floor. Danny arranged them in a square. "This is a house."

Noah contemplated that.

"Let's make a roof."

She laid one block on top of the wall. Noah added another.

"Wow, look at that!" Renata said.

Noah leaned forward and, with a swat of the hand, knocked the house down. He flashed Danny a devilish grin.

"Hah! You're a little trouble maker." She buried her face in Noah's chest and pushed him backwards onto the carpet. Noah laughed and laughed.

* * *

While Renata put Noah down for a nap, Danny stayed on the floor pulling out blocks.

"I used to build mazes out of these," she said, when Renata came in from the bedroom. "I'd spend hours laying them out."

"You didn't play with dolls?" Renata asked.

"I'd have them walk through the maze. They'd get stuck and have to go back and figure out another route."

"Weird."

"That's what my mother thought."

She laid the blocks out, building dead ends, through passages, more dead ends. Renata got up and kissed the top of her head.

"Put these away before you come to bed."

"I will."

"You'll figure the school thing out. Just be patient."

Chapter 30

Through the kitchen window, Hurley watched Danny, dressed in puffy ski jacket and black watch cap, stretch a tape measure from the front of her house into the yard. Noah played beside her, "measuring" the front door stoop with a stick.

"What's she up to, now?" Hurley said.

Opal came beside him. "Maybe she wants to build a porch."

"In the middle of December?"

"She's probably restless."

He twirled his toothpick. "I told Buddy way back when he ought to build a porch. Leanne was against it."

"She never liked sitting outside," Opal said. "Air conditioning's done that to people."

He donned his coat and hat. "I'm gonna walk on over."

"Don't you interfere."

He crossed the driveway and knelt down before Noah. "What are you up to, little fella?"

Noah held out his stick.

"Is that your yardstick? Are you going to measure something?"

Noah smiled. "Yes."

Hurley turned to Danny. "You fixing to build a porch?"

"Not exactly. I'm thinking of a solar greenhouse."

"Solar?"

"Yeah, like the sun," Danny said.

She explained about the article she'd read in *Popular Mechanics.*

"It's designed mostly to cut your heating bills, but you can grow plants in it, too. It'd be perfect here. South-facing brick wall to hold the heat. Doorway to vent it into the living room..."

"You want to cover up your front door?"

"We never use it."

He looked up at the big poplar in the yard. "What about that tree?"

"I'm not worried about that," Danny said. "It'll let most of the light through in the winter and shade the glass in the summer."

She ran her hand across the brick siding. "What I want to know is how to attach an angled glass wall to this."

He scratched his ear. "You're going to need a header to hang some rafters. Gonna need a foundation."

"Can you help me build it? I'd like to do it over Christmas break."

* * *

As the pale sun cleared the ridge line across Hope Valley, Danny swung the mattock into the lawn. The blade barely penetrated the clay soil.

"Told you that ground would be hard," Hurley said. "You ought to wait until spring when it softens up."

Danny took another whack, reached down to retrieve her fallen cap. "I can do it."

For the next hour, she labored on the trench, following the string outline that Hurley had laid out. Six feet out from the house, the mattock clinked against something hard. She leaned over and pulled a rusted tool from the dirt.

"Vice grips," she said. "These must be Buddy's."

He reached out. "Lemme see." He turned them over in his hands. "These are mine. Buddy borrowed 'em off me about ten years ago. He swore he'd put 'em back."

"Oh, he's gonna catch hell now," Danny said.

She went back to whacking at the dirt, stopping only to catch a breath and shed another layer of clothes.

When the trench was roughed out, he showed her how to level it using a clear hose filled with colored water. Each of them held an upturned end of the hose at the corners of the trench. Danny scraped and packed the trench until the water rose to the same point. By the end of the day, the trench was finished.

On a 60 degree day in mid-December, he and Danny poured the footing. They mixed the concrete in his wheelbarrow and shoveled it into the trench. He said a colored masonry crew could lay the cinderblock foundation in a couple of hours, but Danny insisted on doing it herself. She finished the wall in two days.

A week before Christmas, he was showing Danny where to drill holes for the header when Buddy's truck sputtered up the drive. He stepped out with a shy smile and a pair of gift-wrapped boxes.

"I come with the presents for you and Opal."

Hurley nodded over his shoulder. "Put 'em inside under the tree."

Buddy hesitated. "What are you building?"

"Solar greenhouse."

"A what?"

Danny explained to him about the addition.

"You're going to cover up the front door?" Buddy said.

He went inside to deposit the presents then came back out to get a closer look at the work on his old house. Hurley reached into his toolbox and presented him with the rusted vice grips. "Recognize these?"

Buddy turned them over. "Where'd you find them?"

"Danny dug 'em up right by the house. You were fixing that faucet, remember?"

Buddy mumbled. "Thought I give 'em back to you."

The side door opened and Noah came out dressed in a winter coat and mittens. He showed Buddy his plastic hammer. Buddy laughed. "You fixing to help?"

"Yeah!" Noah banged on the sill plate, looked at Buddy and grinned. Seconds later, he dropped the hammer and ran out in the yard.

"Don't lose those, now," Buddy said.

Danny called for a break. She sat down next to Buddy, asked him about his work.

"It's picking up," Buddy said. "We're working on that hospital addition at Duke."

"Thank God for Duke. Love 'em or hate 'em, they've got the money."

"Ain't it the truth."

Hurley grew impatient. He glanced at the sun, already sinking into the trees behind the house. "Let's get this header up," he said. "Hand me that drill."

He climbed the footstool and started drilling through the wall, the bit turning ever slower as it sunk into the brick.

"I got a bigger drill than that, Pa," Buddy said. "I can go over to the house and get it."

"Time you come back from the other side of town, we'll be through."

Buddy watched. Finally, he ambled back to the truck. "Y'all need any help, you call me."

When the truck was out of sight, Danny turned to him.

"You ought to let Buddy help you," she said.

"I don't need his help."

"He might need for you to ask him."

When the header was up, he returned to his house. Opal was standing before the Christmas tree putting up decorations.

"Buddy drop his presents by?" he asked.

"There over on the couch," Opal said. "I hate that they're not coming over. I know they want to see Leanne's folks."

"They're coming in the afternoon, aren't they?"

"I guess."

He sat on the couch and picked up the boxes.

"Bud was curious about that greenhouse," Opal said.

"Wha'd he say?"

"He was wondering whose idea it was. I told him it was Danny's. He said it would sure change the look of that house."

He put the present down. "Danny said I ought to have let Buddy help us."

"He offered?"

"He said we ought to use his drill. I told him it was too far to drive."

Opal turned. "I think Danny was right. Bud doesn't live there anymore, but he might have felt better if he could've helped out. He sees how you and Danny have taken a liking to each other. That's got to be hard on him considering."

* * *

The greenhouse was finished on New Years Day. It looked a bit like a spaceship to Hurley, but he was proud of the work they'd done. Danny and Renata were so excited they scheduled an open house for all their friends, Opal and he included.

The day of the party, they stepped into a crowded family room. Opal clutched a poinsettia, which Renata urged her to bring into the greenhouse. He looked around the room in hopes of recognizing some of the guests. There in the kitchen talking with Danny was Omar.

An old fear welled up inside him—black man flirting with white woman. Miscegenation. But as he watched them converse, his feeling became jumbled. These were the two "fathers"—one biological, the other practical. Both of them queer.

Noah came waddling into the kitchen with a toy and held it up for Omar to examine. Omar beamed. "Hey, what do you have there?"

"Tape."

"A tape measure? Man, that is really cool."

The affection between them was disarming. He was still staring, when Omar looked his way. "Hey, Mr. Cates. Good to see you."

They shook hands.

"Man, you did a bang up job on that greenhouse," Omar said.

Hurley thanked him. There were a dozen questions he wanted to ask—what were you doing fathering a child you don't plan to take care of? How do you feel about two women raising your boy? He asked him about his dancing.

"Man, we have been all over the *world*," Omar said. "It's just crazy."

Renata came in the kitchen, eager to show him the greenhouse. She took him by the hand and led him through the crowd. He loved when she did that, gave him special treatment.

As he stepped through what used to be the front door, the sunlight hit him. Through the slanted glass windows, he could see the poplar branches shaking in the winter wind. Here in the greenhouse, it was warm as toast. The aroma of orchids filled the air.

"People brought us all kinds of plants," Renata said. "I have no idea how to care for them."

"Them orchids never last," he said. "You best enjoy them while you can."

He looked around the space. "Are you going to plant you some tomato seedlings?"

"I'll get a head start on you."

He laughed. "I guess you will."

He studied her face. "I seen Omar in there."

"Yes, I saw you two talking."

"Danny don't mind him being around?"

"No, Danny loves Omar."

"Does Noah know he's his Daddy?"

"No. He just things he's a friend."

"Are you gonna tell him?"

"I don't know. Maybe when he's older."

He shook his head. These people were mighty brave or mighty stupid, he wasn't sure which. He couldn't believe that he would ever be accepting of such a thing. But in this moment, in this warm, bright space that he helped create, anything seemed possible.

Chapter 31

As springtime came and Noah approached a year-and-a-half, Hurley found his affections for the boy growing. Noah called him by name—Gapaw—just like Ricky and L. Dog. For all practical purposes, he was his Grandpa. If he or Opal was on the porch and the neighbors came outside, Noah insisted on coming over. He would waddle across the drive and climb up the steps on all fours. It was always a tussle between him and Opal to see who could lure him to their lap first.

Ricky and L. Dog liked him. Of course, they wanted to know why he was black. Opal told them he'd been adopted. At first, Noah was too small to play in any of their games, but as the summer went on and the boy became surer on his feet, he watched them with growing eagerness.

On a Sunday in September, Dwayne and Dawn left the boys with Hurley and Opal so they could go see a movie. While he and Opal sat on the porch, Ricky and L. Dog set out the bases for a kickball game.

"The tire swing is home," Ricky said. "I'm up first."

L. Dog rolled the beach ball to his older brother, who booted it high and hard. It looked like a sure base hit, but L. Dog was turning into a speedy fellow. He ran underneath it and caught it for an out.

Ricky threw up his hands. "Oh, man! That's not fair."

"He's trying harder than you," Hurley said from his rocker. "Ain't nothing to do with fair."

The door opened across the drive. Renata and Noah came out. When he saw Hurley, Noah broke into a bow-legged run. "Gapaw, look!"

"Hey, boy, what you got there?"

"A sword."

"A sword? Where'd you get that?"

Renata strode onto the porch and sat in the swingseat. "We got it at the circus. He spotted them the minute we walked in."

Noah crawled up the steps and held the sword out to him. "Push it."

Hurley pushed the button on the hilt and the plastic blade lit up. "How 'bout that?"

Ricky and L. Dog stopped their game and came up to examine the sword.

"That's not real," Ricky said.

He frowned. "Boy!"

"It's not."

Noah dropped his sword and leaned against Hurley.

"Oh, well," Renata said. "The magic was bound to fade."

Opal clapped her hands at Noah. "Come see Gamaw."

He pushed away and climbed into Opal's lap. "It's hard being the smallest, isn't it?" she said.

Noah nodded. Opal kissed him on top of his head. "Buddy was smaller than the other boys his age," she said to Renata. "They picked on him something awful."

"Buddy was a cry baby," he said.

"He didn't get much help," Opal snapped. "You were too busy with your chores."

He knew better than to respond. There was no point in explaining that a man had things he needed to do. Children on a farm needed to be responsible for themselves.

"I worry about that for Noah," Renata said. "He might be the only mixed race boy in his class."

"He can take care of himself, can't you, Sword Boy?"

Danny came outside and joined the others on the porch.

"Are you back to school?" Opal asked.

Danny nodded. "Since mid-August."

"Did they give you that tenure yet?"

She shook her head. "No, but this is the year. I either get it or I'm out of there."

He spat. "I don't go for that tenure. You ought to be held responsible your whole life."

"It's not like you can't get fired," Danny said. "It just makes it more difficult. The big thing is the pay. I can't afford to stay on as an assistant."

"How much are they paying you?"

"$35,000."

"That's as much as I ever made at American Tobacco and I worked there 45 years."

"You didn't have the education," Opal said. "They pay you more if you've been to college."

He spat again. Renata rose to her feet.

"I need to go to the grocery store," she said to Danny. "Will you watch Noah?"

"Sure."

"Do you have anything you want to add to the list?"

"Beer."

Opal rose from her chair. "I need to get supper going. Y'all stay put."

When Opal and Renata had gone, Noah climbed down the steps and hung through the tire swing, watching Ricky and L. Dog run the bases.

"You boys let Noah play," Hurley said.

Ricky frowned. "He's too small."

"Roll it to him easy."

Ricky positioned Noah in front of the tire swing. "Stand right here."

He rolled the ball. It hit Noah in the chest.

"Kick it!" L. Dog shouted.

Noah took a little hop. The ball went nowhere.

"See?" Ricky said.

Danny suggested they try some other game. Ricky and L. Dog conferred.

"Let's play war," Ricky said. "Can we get the guns, Gapaw?"

"Go get 'em," he said. "Stay away from Gamaw's dolls."

Ricky and L. Dog ran inside and came back out with two plastic rifles. Ricky instructed Noah to use his sword. Together they took up positions, Ricky and L. Dog behind the tree, Noah behind the tire swing.

Danny smiled. "Noah's in heaven. He never gets to play war."

Every time a car passed on the road, Ricky gave the order to fire. He and L. Dog aimed their guns and made shooting noises. Noah did the same with his sword.

Hurley laughed. "His sword just changed into a rifle."

Ricky cried out as an imaginary army charged up the hill. "Fall back! Fall back!"

They disappeared around the side of the house.

"Football started yet?" he asked Danny.

"At Duke? I have no idea. Actually, I have one football player in my class. He's the one that sleeps in the back."

"Is he white or black?"

"He's black."

He thought to make some comment about blacks being admitted to Duke just for their athletic ability, then thought the better of it. Noah was a smart boy, smarter than Buddy was at his age. He might even go to Duke some day.

The door closed across the drive and Renata came out with her grocery list. She'd just driven past the front porch when she slammed on her brakes. She called out the window, "Where are the boys?"

Danny stared across the yard. In no time, Renata was out of the car and striding across the lawn. "They were right here a minute ago," Danny said.

She trotted past the porch calling Noah's name. Out of the barn, Ricky and L. Dog came running. "He's in there," Ricky said.

Renata ran inside and, seconds later, came out dragging Noah by the arm. She glared at Danny. "I leave him with you for five minutes and you let him out of your sight."

Danny hung her head.

"They knocked over your scythe, Hurley," she said. "It's a miracle no one got hurt."

Renata loaded Noah into the car and sped out the drive. Danny started down the steps. "I guess the party's over. See you tomorrow."

Chapter 32

In mid-December, Renata's mother became ill. Renata and Danny had to make a last minute trip to Florida and didn't want to have to deal with Noah in the hospital. They asked Opal if she and Hurley would mind taking Noah for the weekend. She jumped at the chance.

Friday morning, Renata brought Noah and a collection of gear—a portable crib, a bag of clothes, diapers, toys, a stack of books.

"He'll eat pretty much anything that isn't spicy," Renata said.

She smiled. "That sounds like Hurley."

When the front door closed, Noah started to cry. She picked him up and carried him into the living room. "We're going to have a good time," she said. "Just you wait."

"I can show him the tool drawer," Hurley said.

She frowned. "Go set up his crib. Let me have some time with him."

Noah looked around the living room. He saw the glass case with her figurines. "This," he said.

She sighed. "I knew you were going to want to see the Hummels."

She set Noah on the floor and retrieved the key from the side of the cabinet. "These are Gamaw's Hummels," she said. "We have to be real careful with them or they might break."

She unlocked the glass door. "Which one do you want?"

Noah studied the figurines. He pointed to the little girl with the outstretched hand holding a glass diamond. She set the figurine on the living room table. "Pretty, isn't she?"

"She's crying," Noah said.

She studied the girl's expression. "Maybe she wants people to see her pretty diamond."

Noah pondered for a moment, then turned back to the case. "That one."

"Hold on a minute. Let's put this one back."

Hurley came in from the bedroom. "How's he doing?"

"He's going to want to see them all."

"Let him help you with the cookies."

Making Christmas cookies had been one of the activities she considered for entertaining Noah. Patsy and Buddy had both loved it, but she couldn't remember how old they were when they started. She put the footstool by the counter and helped Noah up. While she prepared the dough, he played with the tin cookie cutters, choosing the gingerbread man to make the first cookie.

She showed him how to press the cutter into the dough. She peeled the man off the wax paper and put him on the cookie sheet. Noah's dark eyes crinkled.

"Will you look at that smile?" she said.

Hurley laughed. "He's having a good time, now."

Noah pressed out a dozen more figures. When they were all on the cookie sheet, Opal handed him the bottle with the pink sprinkles. "Just shake it a bit. You want some on each cookie."

Noah shook the bottle hard, sprinkles landing all over the counter and the floor.

"Oh, Lord."

By noon, she was exhausted. She fed Noah lunch and put him down for a nap. "I don't know that I can stand five days of this," she said to Hurley.

"Why don't we take him to the mall in the afternoon?" he said. "Show him that Christmas display?"

She pondered that idea. The last time she'd gone was with Ricky and L. Dog. They'd marveling at how the fake bear was able to talk with the audience.

"I suppose."

After Noah awoke from his nap, they bundled him up and drove to the mall. The place was crowded with Christmas shoppers.

Hurley frowned. "Lotta colored in here."

Just navigating through the crowd was nerve-wracking enough, but the stares thrown their way frightened Opal. Some were curious, others hostile. She held tight to Noah's hand, wishing she'd brought a hat to cover his curly head.

They reached center court and found the Christmas display. This year it was a life-sized group of angels, their mouths frozen in song. "Joy to the World" boomed through the hidden speakers. She brought Noah right to the edge.

"Those are angels," she said. "Do you know what they are?"

Noah shook his head.

"They live up in heaven with God. They watch over little children like you."

"Are they real?"

"Not those."

Around the perimeter of the display, children watched wide-eyed. But more than a few of the adults stared at the elderly white couple with the brown boy. When the song was over, Noah turned to Opal. "I want to go home."

On the ride home, she was silent, realizing for the first time what it felt like to be stared at because of your color. Had Noah sensed it? Was that why he wanted to go home?

She glanced at the sleeping boy in his car seat.

"That walk must have tuckered him out," she said.

Hurley glanced in the mirror. "He don't like the crowds."

That evening, she and Noah sat on the couch looking through his collection of books. They were all a series she didn't recognize. *Berenstain Bears.* He picked one out for her to read, *The Berenstain Bears New Neighbors.* It told how a family of Pandas moved in next door, how Papa bear incorrectly assumed that their row of bamboo was a "spite fence." Over his objections, the cubs befriend the Pandas and proved to their father that, despite their differences, the neighbors were worthy of love and respect.

"That's an interesting book," she said to Noah.

Hurley came in and stood before Noah. "How'd you like to go out in the field and cut a Christmas tree tomorrow? We'll get my ax out of the tool shed. You can bring your sword."

Noah sat up. "Yeah!"

"Don't get him too excited," she said. "He won't get to sleep."

"He needs to get outside in the woods."

After breakfast, they set out walking on the tractor path to the back field. The sky was a flat gray, the forest a lifeless brown. But Noah ran ahead swinging his sword as if it was the first day of spring.

When they reached the field, Hurley paused to scan the edges where the young cedars grew. She and Noah followed him across the uneven ground until he found one to his liking.

"You like this one, Noah?"

"Yeah!"

"That's awful big," she said. "It'll probably touch the ceiling."

"I want that one!"

Hurley winked. "I guess we better get it."

He took a whack at the tree, the ax bouncing off of the springy trunk. He swung again at a sharper angle. When the tree finally sagged over, Noah ran up and claimed it. He turned to Opal with a serious face. "This is a Cwistmas twee."

When he got back to the house, Hurley brought the stand out of the attic and erected the tree in the living room. She gathered the boxes of decorations from the hall closet. One by one, she and Noah unwrapped the treasures—the glass balls, the icicles, the angels—and hung them on the tree. The last item they opened was the creche.

"This is the baby Jesus," Opal said. "You don't know who he is, do you?"

He shook his head.

Opal sighed. "He's the whole reason we *have* Christmas."

It bothered her that Noah had no understanding of Jesus, of why we celebrate his birth. As long as he was under Danny and Renata's roof, he never would.

She checked her watch. There was still another two hours before Danny and Renata were due back. While Hurley watched television, she led Noah to Bud and Patsy's old room. In the bookshelf, she found *The Child's Story Bible.*

"Come sit beside me on the bed and I'll read you a story."

She turned to the chapter on Genesis 6, 7, and 8 and explained about the people who lived a long time ago. She told how God had become angry with all the people in the world because they had forgotten about Him. They did not pray to Him or ask His forgiveness. God was so angry that he decided to create a flood that would cover the Earth.

"But there was one good man in the world, and God did not want to destroy him. The man's name was Noah."

She checked to see that Noah was paying attention. "That's your name, isn't it?"

He nodded.

"God told Noah to build a ship so that he and his sons and his wife's sons might be saved from the flood. He told them they must bring to the ship two of every kind of animal—beasts, and birds, and creeping things—to keep them alive and to start a new world after the flood."

Noah pulled his thumb out of his mouth. "Gus?"

Opal frowned. "What?"

"Did Gus come?"

"No, Gus didn't live that long ago."

She went on to explain that Noah's neighbors thought he was very foolish to build the ark when there was no sign at all of any flood. But Noah trusted God and kept on gathering all the different animals.

"When they were all safe in the ark, God sent the rain."

Chapter 33

Just before spring break, Danny got the news. Tenure. She was utterly surprised, which made it all the better. People she'd thought badly of now seemed wise and kind. She stepped from the office into the glorious sunshine, the dogwoods on campus in full bloom, students in flip flops and shorts.

On the way home, she picked up Noah from the sitters and got a bottle of champagne from the grocery store. She put the champagne on ice and waited. Six o'clock passed, Renata's normal arrival time, then six fifteen. Noah whined that he was hungry.

"Mommy's late from work," she said. "I'll feed you."

She started the water for spaghetti and poured the sauce in the pot. By six-thirty, Renata was still not home. She served Noah his dinner, poured herself a glass of wine. At 7 o'clock, Renata strolled in wearing a dreamy smile.

"Where the heck have you been?" Danny said.

Renata's smile faded. "I was having drinks with people from work. I told you I was going to do that."

"I don't remember you saying anything."

"I did. You were taking Noah out of his highchair."

She thought back to the morning rush. Maybe Renata did say something. "Where'd you go?"

"Governor's Inn."

Renata shed her coat. She was wearing the tight-fitting sleeveless skirt and black stockings. She came up to Noah and kissed him on the forehead. "How's my little boy? Are you getting enough dinner?"

"Who'd you go out with?" Danny said.

"Carol, Cathy, James."

James. Danny'd been to office parties where James was present. She saw the way he looked at Renata. As if she were fair game. A lesbian partner didn't count. But enough of that.

"I got it," she said.

Renata looked up. "What?"

"Tenure."

Renata gasped. "Oh, my God." She ran forward and embraced her. "I told you to be patient. That is so wonderful."

They kissed. They kissed again. "I'm sorry I blew up at you," she said. "I forgot you were going out."

"That's alright. I should have reminded you."

"Can I make it up to you?"

Renata smiled. "I suppose."

Danny put Noah to bed and found Renata in the bedroom. They undressed each other standing up, Danny unclipping Renata's stockings and sliding them down her legs. Renata shook them free, laughing like a girl. She lay back on the bed and Danny went down on her, tonguing her side to side the way she liked. Renata moaned, "Now. Please." Danny got the dildo from the bedside table. She lay face to face with Renata, eased the dildo inside her.

"Do you want to give him a name?" she whispered.

"What?"

"Do you want to give our friend a name? You can call him anything you want. I don't care."

Renata closed her eyes, panting.

"Anything you want," Danny breathed.

Just then, the door opened. Renata grabbed the sheets and pulled them up to her chin. Noah stood with tears running down his cheeks. "I wet the bed."

Chapter 34

Summertime and the living was easy. Opal sat on the porch with Hurley, watching Danny mow the lawn with Noah in her lap. They rode up and down, he with his hands on the wheel, a look of utter seriousness on his face. It reminded her of the days when Hurley did that with Patsy and Buddy. What a thrill that must be for a child to feel in control of a big machine, to watch the grass come at you tall and ragged and leave short and smooth.

Renata came out to watch. Hurley called her over like he usually did. Opal knew he was sweet on her, and that was fine. Everybody's allowed a little dream.

"Noah's having a big time out there," she said, as Renata settled into the swing seat.

"It makes me nervous to see that," Renata said. "I worry Danny's going to drop him."

"He's alright," Hurley said. "I used to do that with Patsy and Buddy when they were that age."

"I'm sure you did. You probably let them drive the car."

When Danny finished, she steered the rider over to the porch and parked underneath the forked oak. Noah got down and strode up the steps like a big man.

"Did you just mow that lawn?" Hurley said.

He went over to Renata. "Yes."

"With your momma?"

"No," he said, patting Renata. "This is one's momma. That one's mom."

Danny climbed up the stairs and sat on a rocker. "So you're mom and she's momma," Opal said.

Danny nodded. "That's what we decided."

Noah strode over to Opal. "Did you have a momma and a mom?"

"No, I had a momma and a daddy."

"Why?"

She laughed. "I guess because they liked each other."

Noah trotted away and climbed in Danny's lap.

"Which one of you does the cooking?" Hurley said. "I know Danny does the lawn."

"I usually do the cooking, unless it's on the grill," Renata said. "Danny does the household chores."

"She does the laundry," Danny said.

It was a wonder how those two worked things out. She had to admit that she didn't believe two women could lead a normal life together, much less raise a child. But they seemed happy, and Noah seemed happy. It made her sad in a way, thinking how things might have been for Patsy. She might have been able to find a friend. Not have a child, but at least have a friend to love. Instead, they made her feel ashamed, made her hide.

Chapter 35

August, Hurley knew, marked the start of hurricane season in the Carolinas. The weather man would show pictures of storms developing in the Caribbean, white shapes that looked like big pinwheels. Usually, they petered out or turned away from the mainland. Sometimes, they'd run along the coast, bust up some houses and flood Highway 12. But Adelaide was different. It was big. It was powerful. And it was on track to run right up the middle of the state.

Two days before the storm was scheduled to hit, he and Opal went through the house, taking an inventory of supplies. They had one bottle of lamp oil and a half-dozen D cell batteries. He would get more of those tomorrow.

Monday morning, the hardware store was full of people roaming the aisles, grabbing up some of everything. They'd have to go through a storm before they knew what all they needed. The D cell batteries were already gone from the rack by the front, but he knew the store kept some extras in Electrical. Before the jealous stares of the customers, he carried the last pack to the cash register.

"And I'll get two bags of ice," he said.

The day before the storm, the hill was quiet. He and Opal picked all the corn that was ready. Those skinny stalks wouldn't tolerate a wind. They sat on the back patio shucking the husks into a paper bag. He noticed a trembling in Opal's hands.

"How long you had that shake?"

"It's been coming on about a week now."

"You ought to see the doctor."

"I'm just getting old."

After dinner, Danny came over and sat on the porch.

"Y'all ready for the storm?" Hurley asked.

"I think so. We've got a flashlight and some candles."

"I like me a lantern. Gives off more light than a candle."

Renata came up the drive. She waved and carried Noah into the house.

"What did you teach your students today?" he asked.

"We were discussing the invention of hell."

"Invention?"

"It's actually a fairly recent concept. The Greeks and Romans didn't even have a word for it."

"Bible tells about it."

"It showed up when the Romans started persecuting the Jews. The theory is the Jews had to believe their tormentors would be punished, so they came up with the notion of hell. The Christians took the idea and embellished it to suit their own needs."

He gave his smile. "You don't believe in hell?"

* * *

Tuesday evening, the leaves began to rustle. Birds darted back and forth between the trees. From the front porch, he and Opal watched a raft of clouds sail in from the north.

"I thought this was coming from the south," she said.

He spat. "It's spinning like a wheel. We're just seeing the top of it."

He studied the forked oak, its tire swing slung from a limb the size of a telephone poll. For sixty years, it had shaded the house, but a big wind could blow it down. With the weight of those limbs it would go right through the roof.

By the time he and Opal were ready to turn in, the sky had turned yellow-green. All the trees were in motion, speaking in tongues. He sniffed the air.

"You smell that?" he said.

Opal paused at the door. "Smells like we're down at the coast."

"That's salt blown all this way. Two hundred miles."

He took a last look at the hill. The lawn, the trees, the barn, the sheds—everything looked just as he wanted. But the world was not made for him. Best to close the door and pray the storm passed them by.

Inside, Opal sat on the bed, rubbing arthritis cream on her hands. "Did you bring the porch chairs in?"

"I put 'em in the living room."

"I hope we don't lose too many branches." She switched off the light and, turning towards the wall, pulled the covers over her shoulder. As he did every night, Hurley snuggled up to her backside. He rested his chin against her spine, his hand on her hip.

* * *

He awoke to a sound like someone spraying the roof with a garden hose. It came in surges, loud and hard.

"Sounds like it's hailing," Opal said.

He thought the same, then realized it was something else. "That ain't hail. It's acorns coming down."

He got out of bed and looked under the shade. Against the cloud-blackened sky, the pines at the wood's edge swung in crazy circles. How much could they take before they snapped?

"Come on back to bed," Opal pleaded.

He lay on his back, staring at the ceiling. The roof creaked. It had never done that before. He thought back sixty years to when the carpenters built this house. They'd used 20 penny nails and real 2x6 rafters, bigger than what's used on houses these days. But even that might not be enough.

From the woods came the sound of limbs cracking. He tried to gauge the location. This one over by the barn, that one behind Danny and Renata's. Suddenly, there was a loud pop overhead. He held his breath. The ground shook.

He tried switching on the lamp. "Power's out."

Opal sat up. "Oh, Lord."

He felt for the flashlight. "I need to see where that branch hit."

He cracked open the front door and felt a rush of wind suck the air from his lungs. It took him a moment to realize that the rattling wall of leaves blocking his view was the forked oak.

Above the howl of wind, he thought he heard the wailing of a child. He aimed the beam of the flashlight out the end of the porch and saw Danny and Renata come running across the lawn with Noah.

"Go 'round back!" he called. "The steps is blocked."

He hurried through the house and unlocked the kitchen door. Danny and Renata pushed their way in.

"A tree came through our fucking ceiling," Danny said. "I thought we were going to die."

Noah moaned in Renata's arms. "I'm scared."

"It's alright, baby," she said. "We're O.K. now."

He struck a match and lifted the globe. The wick burned bright, emitting a plume of smoke. Faces emerged from the dark. Danny, Renata, and Noah were all in their pj's, the wet cotton clinging to their skin.

"What's that in your hair?" Hurley pulled a pink tuft from Renata's hair. Insulation.

"Oh my God," she said. "That came from our ceiling. There was this huge bang and then this shower of stuff."

Opal appeared from the bedroom. "Is everyone alright? Lord, you're soaked clean through. I'll get some towels."

Renata looked down, pulled the thin cotton top away from her breasts.

"We lost power," Danny said. "I couldn't find our raincoats."

Opal arrived with towels and wrapped up Noah. "Come see Gamaw," she said. "You've got on your Superman pajamas. Are you going to save the world?"

Noah buried his face in Opal's shoulder.

"What are we going to do?" Danny asked him. "The rain is pouring into our bedroom."

"Nothing you can do until this storm passes," he said. "Just sit tight."

"Y'all can stay in the guest room," Opal said. "It's just twin beds. I'll get you some dry clothes."

He lit a second lantern and led the way to the guest bedroom.

"This used to be Patsy's room," he said.

Rain beat on the roof. The rafters shook again. Renata stared at the black-and-white-portrait on the wall.

"Is this Patsy?" she said.

He nodded.

"She looks like you."

Opal came in with Noah. She stood him on the floor, stripped off his pajamas, and wrapped him in a towel. "Let's dry you off and get you in bed."

Noah whined. "I don't have clothes."

"We'll get you some tomorrow."

She slipped his brown, naked body under the covers, and kissed his forehead.

Hurley set the lamp on the bedside table and followed Opal to the door. He looked back, a feeling of warmth flooding his chest. All here now, under one roof.

Chapter 36

At first light, he looked out the bedroom window. The clouds were giving way to blue sky. Opal was still asleep, the covers pulled tight around her narrow shoulders, so he dressed quietly in his khaki work shirt and pants and headed for the front door.

The warm, moist air bore the trademark odor of cut red oak—cat piss. Sure enough, the left half of the forked oak had split and fallen against the porch. The rest was still standing, the massive cream-colored scar oozing sap.

He walked to the end of the porch and stared across the drive. The poplar in Danny and Renata's front yard had blown over, smashing the solar greenhouse and going part way through the roof. Only the brick walls had kept it from going all the way through.

In Danny and Renata's backyard, the two pines that anchored the woodpile had been uprooted and were hung up in an oak tree above the car shed.

Opal stepped out in her robe. Her hand went to her mouth. "Oh, Lord."

He shook his head. "Fix me some breakfast so I can get to work."

When Hurley rolled back the barn door, Gus was waiting. The dog spun in circles, yipping.

"Hey, boy, you glad to see me? Yes, you are." For the first time ever, he let the dog lick him in the face.

As Hurley walked back to the house, Gus darted onto the lawn to sniff the clusters of leaves and twigs. The sky shone blue, the air fresh, but the woods were devastated, trees leaning and broken. It'd be years before it came close to normal again. There was no greater plan. There were coons dead inside their trees, while others gorged themselves on fallen fruit. None of it made any sense.

Danny came out dressed in a pair of his long pants and sleeveless undershirt. Renata followed in Opal's overcoat, Noah in his Superman pajamas. "Let's see what this done to your house," Hurley said.

Noah ran into the back yard and stood before the toppled pines. The rootballs, still attached to the ground by the big taproot, loomed like giant spiders over the water-filled craters.

"Stay away from there," Renata said.

Inside, the family room lay untouched, a plug-in flashlight sitting unopened on the kitchen counter. Renata looked in the greenhouse. The poplar had smashed two of the angled panes, beads of glass covered the planting beds and floor.

"This is ruined," she said.

He stuck his head in. "That's the trouble with a skylight."

Danny called from the bedroom. "Wait'll you see this."

Renata picked up Noah and together they went down the darkened hall to the master bedroom doorway. Inside, the queen bed was littered with drywall chips and tufts of pink insulation. Two cracked rafters poked through the ceiling. Above them lay the trunk of the poplar.

Danny shook her head. "We could have been killed."

She pulled back the sheets and felt the mattress. "It's soaked."

"Forget that mattress," he said. "First thing you need to do is nail a tarp over that roof, keep your floor from getting ruined if it rains again. I got one out in the barn you can borrow. Then you got to find a tree man and a roofer."

"What do you think it'll cost to fix this?" Renata said.

"It'll cost your insurance man plenty," he said. "It won't cost you a dime. Those trees over the car shed are another matter. Your homeowner's probably won't cover that because they didn't do any damage. But you need to have them taken down before they do."

Renata and Danny turned toward each other, their faces crumpling at once. They embraced each other in the ruined bedroom and cried.

Chapter 37

Opal opened the refrigerator and pulled out the freezer drawer. "We better eat this bacon before it goes bad. That and the eggs. It might be the rest of the week before the power comes on."

Hurley opened the cooler and poured in the bags of ice. "Hand me that milk and whatever else will fit."

After breakfast, he set to work on the broken half of the forked oak. He started at the top, cutting the leafy branches, putting them in the wheelbarrow and hauling them to the woods. He cut the thicker branches into woodstove length and hauled those to the barn and started a new woodpile.

Amidst the tangle, he found the tire swing, its rope knotted to the lowest branch. The day he tied it up, Patsy and Buddy had swung on it all day long, spinning each other until they fell down dizzy. He cut the rope and tossed it and the tire into the wheelbarrow.

Finally, he started into the trunk. The big oak swallowed the 20-inch blade. He had to cut from both sides, and by the time the first piece dropped free, the saw was smoking. He shut it off and sat on the trunk for a rest.

Across the drive, Danny leaned a ladder against the roof. She and Renata inched their way up, Danny carrying the blue tarp and Renata a pair of hammers. He went over to offer advice.

"Stretch that tarp over the trunk where it goes through the roof, then nail it down."

"Won't that just make more holes?" Renata said.

"You ain't got to worry about those little holes. It's the big one'll do you damage."

While Noah banged the ground with a toy hammer, his parents started swinging the real ones. Renata hit her thumb and cried out, "Ow, that hurts."

He laughed. "You'll hit it again before you're through."

It was two days before women could get their insurance agent over. He told them their policy would pay for the damage to the house, including removal of the poplar, but not for the two pines that hung over the car shed.

It took another week to find a tree company that would do the work and the price they quoted was outrageous—three thousand dollars for the two pines, including removal of the stumps.

"I wouldn't pay that kind of money," he said when they women asked his advice.

"We got three quotes and that was the cheapest one," Renata said.

He studied the two trees where they hung in the crown of the oak. "We might could take those down ourselves," he said. "Buddy's company's got a bucket truck. He might be willing to bring that over."

Renata frowned. "Don't you think we should hire a professional tree remover?"

He spat. "I've cut plenty of trees."

* * *

In the still of the evening, he and Opal sat on the back patio enjoying the last of the daylight. With the power out a week and a half, they had gone back to the rhythms of older times, rising with the dawn, retiring with the dark. The absence of television led to more conversation. Meals were cooked outdoors on the grill and eaten under the trees.

"I'm not sure I agree with your bringing Bud and them all into this tree cutting business," Opal said.

He sniffed. "They'll be alright."

"Those bucket trucks make me nervous."

"It'll be a lot safer than trying to cut it from the ground. Those trees are like to land right on top of that car shed."

The smell of barbecued chicken drifted across the drive. Danny stood on the back deck tending the gas grill. Gus waited beside her for a stray piece to fall his way.

"I kind of like it with the power out," Opal said. "Everything's so quiet."

He smiled. "Summertime, Momma used to wait for the first whippoorwill. That's when she said it was time to come inside."

Noah came out on the deck, climbed on the bench and stabbed his sword at an invisible enemy. "Gyuh! Gyuh!"

"Sword Boy's fighting something," he said.

Opal smiled. "He's a character."

"Chicken's ready," Danny called.

Renata came out with paper plates and set them on the table. She told Noah to put his sword away. The boy cried. "Nooo!"

The light faded, leaving only the outline of the trees. From back in the wood's edge, a birdcall punctuated the stillness. "*Whip-poor-WILL, whip-poor-WILL, whip-poor-WILL.*"

Chapter 38

The truck came rumbling up the drive, its retracted bucket skimming the branches of the overhanging oaks. Buddy stepped out of the cab and unloaded a pair of chainsaws and a length of rope.

The women came out on the deck, Renata holding Noah. "Look at that big truck!" she said to him.

Buddy came over and pinched Noah on the cheek, "You're getting big, boy. How old are you?"

Noah held up his hand and counted the fingers. "Almost free."

Dwayne arrived in his Firebird with Ricky and L. Dog. The boys clambered out with toy rifles in hand.

"Let's play war," Ricky said to Noah. "Go get your sword."

Renata set Noah down. "You boys stay on the deck."

The men studied the pines, laying one atop the other.

"I'll toss a rope over that oak limb and tie it onto those pines," Buddy said. "I'll cut them up in pieces and we can lower them down nice and easy."

Hurley nodded. "We'll need one man to work that rope and another on the roof of the car shed to steer the pieces away."

"I'll get on the roof," Dwayne said. "We don't need you falling off and breaking a leg."

Danny approached. "Anything I can do?"

"Carry them pine branches into the woods after he cuts them off," Hurley said. "It's gonna be a mess of them."

"Please be careful, Danny!" Renata called.

While Dwayne leaned a ladder against the roof, Buddy drove the truck up against the car shed. He climbed into the bucket with a chainsaw and rope and raised himself up toward the trees. He cranked up the chain saw and started cutting into the tangled crowns of the two pines. As he tossed the branches to the ground, Danny hauled them into the woods. Buddy shut off the saw, looped the rope over one of the branches of the oak and tied it to the trunk of the topmost pine.

"Mind that lower pine don't jump up when you cut the top one," Hurley said.

Buddy cranked up the saw and started cutting into the trunk. Piece by piece, he cut up the topmost pine. As each section came free, Hurley lowered them to the ground. Soon, the pine was reduced to a limbless stub tilting up from the root ball.

Renata went inside, satisfied that the operation was safe. Seeing that she was gone, the boys leapt off the deck and ran into the yard. Hurley glimpsed them hiding in the crater beneath one of the rootballs, shooting at some unseen enemy. It was then that he noticed the limbless pine, its taproot still attached to the ground, tilting back upright.

"You boys get out of there!" he yelled.

Ricky scrambled out. L. Dog scrambled out. The rootball closed over the hole.

Chapter 39

As she rode with Hurley, Opal stared at the tops of the trees rushing past on Hope Valley Road. She thought back to the day of Patsy's funeral, how she swung from one emotion to the next—the hopeful words of the preacher, the awful sight of the coffin, the kindness of friends, Hurley's ravaged face. Here she was again, sitting next to her silent husband.

The parking lot to the funeral home was filled to overflowing. "Lord, the whole town's come out," she said.

Hurley spotted Buddy's truck parked on the shoulder and pulled in behind. She checked her purse. "Let me make sure I've got my tissues."

She felt dizzy stepping out of the truck and reached for Hurley's arm. She needed him to be strong now, but his arm hung limp, his hand in his pocket.

A slick-haired boy in a black suit opened the door. They each took a program and stepped inside. The heat of closely packed bodies filled the low-ceilinged room. If Danny and Renata had belonged to a church, they would at least have had a nice sanctuary.

An usher pointed out seats in the back row. They sidled in next to a bearded young man who glanced at Hurley, turned and whispered to his wife.

On the podium, the woman preacher from the wedding sat with a book in hand. Opal hoped it was a Bible, but she couldn't be sure. She scanned the crowd. Three rows up, Buddy stood with Leanne, Dwayne, and the boys. She worried about all of those boys, how responsible each must feel.

Danny and Renata sat in the front row, flanked by their parents. How those two must be suffering. She knew the despair of losing an adult child, but to lose a three-year-old. Could they ever go on with life?

The music started, played by a woman at the electric piano. Opal did not recognize the tune and wondered if this ceremony, like the wedding, was going to be alien to her. The preacher stood, walked to the podium and opened her Bible. "The Lord is my shepherd. He maketh me to lie down in green pastures; he leadeth me beside still waters..."

Thank goodness. Danny and Renata might not call themselves Christians, but when it came to something like this, they knew to turn to the Bible. The preacher finished the reading and addressed the gathering.

"Three years ago, Noah was born to these two loving parents seated before me. I did not know Noah personally, but everyone I have spoken with has told me how beautiful and loving this child was."

Opal glanced at Hurley, his eyes vacant. Was he hearing any of this?

"People we love sometimes die prematurely, and when they do, we are rendered for a time inconsolable. It seems so meaningless and random and unfair. In time, those who have the will and the strength of heart find a way to remember the best attributes of the loved one and integrate those into their own lives so that the deceased's spirit will live on, as it were, in the efforts of the living to carry that spirit forward."

The preacher called forth anyone in the audience who wished to speak. Renata approached the podium and unfolded a sheet of paper, her face dark with fright.

"Five days ago, I lost the most important person in my life. Noah was..." Her hand went to her mouth. She took a breath and started again. "Noah was amazing in so many ways..." She dropped her head and broke into tears.

Opal squeezed Hurley's hand. Somebody help this brave woman.

A small man stood—Renata's father. He walked to the podium and wrapped his daughter in his arms.

"I think my daughter needs to sit for a minute." He led her back to her seat.

Opal expected Danny to speak, but she sat with her arm around Renata. Danny's father stood and approached the podium.

"My memory of my grandson is of a young warrior," he began. "As many of you know, Noah loved his swords."

Gentle laughter coursed through the crowd.

"He was always fighting something in his imagination, defending his hilltop against all foes. But he also loved everyone without reservation. I wonder if we can do that as adults, be strong in defense of what needs defending, but be open and loving at the same time."

He stopped and adjusted his glasses. "I want to say what a terrible accident this was. But we must not lay blame. There is no salvation in that."

She glanced at Hurley. He hadn't said a word about his responsibility, but this whole operation had been his idea. And he took such care in everything he did.

After Danny's father finished, no one else stood to speak. The music started and the family stepped into the aisle. Danny and Renata walked arm in arm, faces wracked with grief. Just as she was about to pass, Renata looked straight at Hurley, eyes filled with rage.

Chapter 40

Danny stared at the cookbook and tried to concentrate. The sound of the nail guns was driving her mad. Pop! Pop! Pop! How long did it take to reshingle a fucking roof? With a shaking hand, she measured the ingredients and stirred in the water.

The knock on the door made her jump. Through the window, she saw the big ears and light bulb head. Buddy.

"Me and Dwayne come for a visit," Buddy said. "Is this a bad time?"

"It's kind of noisy, but you're welcome to come in. I'll get Renata."

She lay on the bed, staring at the ceiling.

"Buddy and Dwayne are here."

Her eyes came into focus. "What do they want?"

"They've come for a visit."

Danny went back to the family room, offered the men some water. They sat on the couch, Buddy holding a Bible.

Renata came in and offered a weak smile. "Hey." She sat at the dining table.

"I see you painted the walls," Dwayne said.

"We did that awhile ago," Renata said.

"I like the white."

"How are they coming on your roof?" Buddy said.

"They said it should be done by the end of the day," Danny said. "I can't wait to get back in the bedroom."

Dwayne cringed as a nail gun opened up overhead. "Dang, that's loud."

"I'd suggest that we go outside, but they've kind of taken over the deck."

"It's O.K." Buddy said. He glanced at Renata. "Ma tells me you've had a lot of visitors."

"It's been non-stop," Renata said. "People have been so kind."

"Times like these, you need your friends."

She managed a smile.

"How are the boys?" Danny said.

"They're pretty shook up. Ricky's the worst. He's just laying around the house."

"Please tell them it's not their fault."

A loud thud shook the roof as the workmen dropped a load of shingles. "Will you tell them to stop?" Renata snapped. "Ask them to come back tomorrow."

Danny went out on the deck and spoke to the crew leader. When she came back inside, Buddy had picked up the Bible.

"I know y'all don't go to church," he said. "And I know it must seem that the Lord is against you. But I believe Noah's in heaven. I believe he's sitting right now with the Lord Jesus Christ."

He opened the Bible to a marked page. "Says here, 'Suffer little children, and forbid them not to come unto me, for such is the kingdom of heaven.' "

"Thank you for reading that," Danny said.

They sat for a moment in silence. "Where's Hurley?" Renata said.

Buddy grimaced. "He's kindly having a hard time."

"Oh?"

"He feels real bad about what happened."

Dwayne nodded. "We ain't never seen a tree do that before. I've had 'em pop up some, but not stand all the way up like that."

Renata glared at him. "That's why you hire a professional."

Chapter 41

Hurley welcomed the shortening days. When darkness came, he could stop thinking about the world outside. He could forget that he had neighbors, that there were tree limbs still in the yard. He could sit in his chair and pretend to watch TV while Opal read the paper.

"State Fair starts this week," she said. "What day do you want to go?"

He spat. "I might skip it."

"You don't want to go to the fair?"

"It's all the same."

He heard the flatness in his voice. Understood its effect on others. But he couldn't do it, couldn't get out of his chair.

"How about we go up to the mountains?" she said. "Paper says the colors are supposed to be good this year."

"Paper always says that."

Opal crunched the paper shut. "Just sit here feeling sorry for yourself, then. You're not the only one that feels bad."

For the first time, he looked up. His wife looked to have aged ten years, her eyes weighed down by heavy bags. He knew she was suffering, too, trying to come up with an answer. It might be good if they left town for awhile.

"What's the name of that creek we fished at down by Linville?" she asked.

"Wilson."

"That was a pretty creek. We could stay in that motel you liked in Boone. Go up on the Parkway."

He pictured the overlooks. There'd be crowds this time of year, but probably they wouldn't run into anyone they knew. Down by the creek, they'd be alone.

* * *

West of Winston-Salem, the highway narrowed to two lanes. The grade rose in long inclines, falling when it crossed a valley, then climbing again over the foothills of the western piedmont. Hurley kept a grip on the wheel, focused on keeping the truck between the lines. Now and again, he glanced at a familiar landmark—the flea market close to the road, the old diner with its hand-painted hot dog and smiling catfish. The paint on the diner had faded. It looked to be closed.

They came over a rise and the flat horizon had transformed to the peaks of the Appalachians.

"There's them mountains," he said.

Opal smiled. "I always forget how big they are."

At the top of every rise, another line of ridges appeared until they were layered six deep, each one higher and bluer than the last.

Finally, the highway began its switchbacked ascent of the Blue Ridge. He pushed the accelerator to the floor. The hazy piedmont fell away like an old coat.

At the crest, they passed under the Blue Ridge Parkway and onto the high plateau. Green meadows flowed beneath marshmallow clouds. Opal pointed to a fiery, red maple in the yard of a farmhouse. "Isn't *that* something?"

He stared at the tree, willing its color to burn through the fog in his mind.

Further on, he spotted dark conical shaped climbing a steep meadow. "Christmas trees, there. Another two months, they'll have 'em down at the shopping center."

"Be nice to buy one this year instead of cutting it."

He pondered that statement. Maybe she was right. A spruce was a nicer tree than a raggedy old cedar.

They drove on through the golden light, arriving at the stoplight in Boone. Across the intersection stood the big colonial structure that housed the Daniel Boone Inn.

"There's that all-you-can-eat place," he said.

Opal brightened. "Remember going there with the children? I wouldn't mind eating there again."

He looked at his watch. "Five o'clock. Time we check into the motel and come back, it'll be six. Like to be a crowd then."

"Why don't we eat now?"

A wall of chatter hit them as they stepped inside. Even at this early hour, the inn was packed. Two couples waited in line before them, a family came up behind them. He was about to suggest they go somewhere else when the hostess called their names. She led them to a table with two other couples, who greeted him and Opal with enthusiastic smiles.

"Have a seat," said a man in a plaid shirt. "Where y'all from?"

"We're from Durham," Opal said.

The man's wife leaned over. "We're from Greenville. We're here to see the colors."

"The best is already gone up high," the man said. "But you'll see some at a lower elevation."

"We were at Grandfather Mountain yesterday," the woman said. "It was just glorious."

"We got halfway out that swinging bridge. She got scared and turned around."

The woman shook her head. "I don't like heights."

A waiter arrived. "It's all you can eat for seven dollars, tea or coffee included. As soon as you finish something, I'll bring a new bowl."

"We been here before," Hurley said.

Within minutes, an army of waiters and waitresses appeared with platters of fried chicken, mashed potatoes, corn, and green beans. Hurley reached for a ham biscuit and wolfed it down. "This here's eatin'," he said.

He loaded his plate and started into the chicken. The skin was not crisp like Opal's. He set it down and picked up an ear of corn. Soggy. He added more pepper and salt, took another bite. Still soggy.

The man looked over. "Did you get much storm damage down your way?"

Hurley pretended to be caught up in eating his corn.

"We had right much," Opal said.

"We lost a couple of big pecans," the woman said. "It just broke my heart."

"Hand me one of them drumsticks," he said to Opal.

A drumstick was usually crisper than a breast, but this one was mushy. Opal had taken only one bite of her corn and was looking at the chicken.

The waiter came by and checked the plates. "Y'all ready for more?"

Hurley shook his head. "I'm full up."

"Hold on, pardner," the man said. "We're just getting started."

He stopped eating and lapsed into silence. The talk grew louder. His heart started to race.

"Carolina's got a good team this year," the woman said. "They got Eric Montross coming back."

"Duke's the team to beat," the man said. "What do you think, Hurley? You're the one from Durham."

He pushed back from the table and addressed Opal. "I'm ready to go."

* * *

The Mountaineer Motel looked smaller and darker than he remembered, the painted logs more old-fashioned. And the sign of the bearded, bow-legged man holding a jug of moonshine looked foolish somehow.

The clerk searched through a card catalogue until he found their name. "Cates. Room 31. That's around back."

"Is there a TV in it?" he asked.

"All our rooms have TVs now."

While Opal unpacked, he lay on the bed and watched the news. It was going to be sunny and cold tomorrow, with a wind chill of 20 degrees.

"That's right cold," Opal said. "Maybe we ought not go to Grandfather."

He sniffed. "Bring a jacket. We won't be up there for long. Be warmer down in the valley by the creek."

In the morning, they stopped at the Wal-Mart so he could get a fishing license and a can of corn. Then, they drove on to the Parkway.

In the space of a hundred yards, the on ramp lifted them above the jumble of roadside attractions into a soft green world of rhododendron and mountain laurel. Autumn leaves spiraled down from dogwood and maple. White pines pointed toward the blue sky.

Mile after mile, the parkway wound in and out of forest and meadow. Now and again, there were overlooks where drivers could pull over and stare into the void. He passed them by.

"You don't want to stop?" Opal asked.

"Nah."

They rounded a bend and there was Grandfather Mountain, its massive eastern flank soaring a thousand feet above the Parkway. Grandfather wore a robe of red and orange, brilliant at the bottom, fading toward the top. Its smooth, stony face was streaked with brown, its shoulders wrapped in a cape of emerald green fir.

"That's a big mountain there," he said.

"The colors are still pretty."

Cars pulled onto the shoulder, passengers jumping out with cameras in hand. He pressed on, heading for the park that led to the Swinging Bridge. He rolled down his window at the entrance.

"That'll be $8," the attendant said.

Hurley frowned. "It was $5 last time I was here."

"That's been the price for ten years, sir."

He wrested the bills from his wallet and drove on to the parking lot. Even with the colors past their peak, the lot was jammed. He found a space in the last row, had to push hard against the car door to overcome the lean of the hill.

Opal tied on her plastic rain bonnet and zipped up her blue blazer. As they reached the top of the parking lot, the wind coming over the ridge blew Opal's bonnet back on her head.

"Lord, it's cold up here," she said.

"Feels good to me."

Along the ridge to the north, tiny figures scaled ladders to reach the top of MacRae's Peak. The sky beyond was a shade of blue he'd never seen in the hazy Piedmont.

Opal turned toward the Visitor's Center. "Do you want to go inside?"

"Let's go on out to the bridge."

The Mile High Swinging Bridge ran from the spine of the mountain to a rock outcropping that teetered over the Linville Valley. It was the big attraction on Grandfather, the place that made you feel you were walking on air. As he and Opal started along the path, families with children streamed past. He took Opal's arm, but she stopped in her tracks.

"You go on out," she said. "It's too windy for me."

He protested, but she was already turned and headed back to the Visitor's Center. He approached the first tower. The walkway looked narrower than he remembered. Maybe he could just look from this side. Caught up in the foot traffic, he found himself pushed onto the bridge. A gust of wind rocked the footpath. He grabbed the rail.

Below him, the ground fell away, 80 feet to the hard rocks. He felt suddenly light-headed. It would be easy to climb the rail. No one would stop him.

"Cold out here," a man said to him. "Winter's on the way."

The mention of winter gave him satisfaction. Everyone would be facing it soon.

He crossed over to Linville Peak and stood on the edge with a dozen others, wind slicing through their jackets. It was a beautiful view, nothing but clear sky all the way over to Tennessee.

As Hurley started back across the bridge, a tow-headed boy approached from the opposite direction. He was holding something out in front of him—a rubber-tipped tomahawk. He marched stiff-legged, eyes unblinking. Hurley froze.

"What did I tell you about that thing?" The father slapped the boy's arm.

The boy started crying.

"I apologize, sir," the man said. "He just got it at the gift shop."

Opal was waiting when he reached the other side. "What's the matter?" she said. "Did you get scared out there?"

He passed without speaking. Opal hurried to catch up.

"Do you want to go to Wilson Creek or do you want to head on back to the motel?" she said. "I'm happy to go back."

"We're going to the creek."

Chapter 42

The gravel road ran for miles, switchbacking down through the hardwood forest.

"Are you sure this is the way?" Opal said. "It's been awhile since we've seen a sign."

"This is it," he said.

The farther they traveled, the less sure he became. In the middle of the woods, all the ridges looked the same. The only thing he was sure of was that they were headed downhill.

Finally, a cluster of cars appeared at a turnout with a trail marker for Wilson Creek. He breathed a sigh of relief, parked the truck and took out the spinning rod and the can of corn. He sat on the tailgate and put on his rubber boots.

Opal read the sign. ".75 miles. That's longer than I want to hike."

"Come on, now. You don't want to be up here by yourself."

"Don't get too far ahead of me."

They started down the trail, Hurley holding the rod out in front. Two switchbacks along, he slipped on the round quartz pebbles that dotted the trail. He caught himself, but the fear that shot up his spine jolted him almost as much as a fall. He called out a warning to Opal and slowed his pace.

A young couple approached with a small brown dog in the lead.

"How much further?" he asked.

"You're about halfway," the woman said.

He doubted that. With all those switchbacks, they had to have walked more than half a mile.

Opal came down, shuffling along at a snail's pace.

"You doing alright?" he said.

"I'll get there on my own time."

Finally, a clearing through the trees. The ground leveled off to where a little girl stood by the stream tossing rocks into a pool and, no doubt, scaring the fish. She ran back to her parents, who were sitting on a log.

"Long way down, ain't it?" he said.

They seemed not to hear him.

"It's getting late," the man said to his daughter. "Let's go on back."

The family left, and he and Opal were alone by the stream. Bright water hissed through gaps in the rocks, and converged into a dark pool where, he was certain, trout were hiding. The mossy boulders were speckled with new-fallen leaves. Down in this lower elevation, much of the canopy was still intact, the arrow-straight trunks of poplar and ash supporting a backlit dome of gold.

He took out his pocket can opener and twisted the lid off the can of corn. He attached a kernel to the bare hook and set the bobber a yard up.

"You want to try a cast?" he said to Opal.

Opal shook her head. "I'll watch."

He waded into the shallows, pressed the button on his reel and flicked the corn into the middle of the current. The bobber drifted untouched. He cast again.

"That girl like to have scared them fish. Let's go on up the trail."

He walked the narrow path to the base of the next pool. This one yielded nothing either. He fished a third pool and a fourth, Opal following him at a distance.

When again he decided to move, she stayed put. "You go on," she said. "I'm happy sitting here."

"I might go up a'ways. This stretch is fished out."

"I'll be alright."

He bypassed the next few runs. Hoisting himself between a pair of boulders, he arrived at the base of a head-high waterfall. He set his rod down and took out his Red Man, all the time watching the spot where the bubbles surged up from the depths. A dark form slender as a leaf rose and fell so quickly one might easily have imagined it. He waited. There it was again—a good-sized trout. He dropped his line in the froth and watched the bobber tumble in the bubbles.

The tug came in an instant, setting his head afire. He pulled back on his rod, felt the quiver of the fish. It tried to flee downstream. He turned it around. "You ain't goin' nowhere, boy." The fish leapt from the dark water—a flash of silver and pink. It darted back and forth in the pool. Within minutes, it was spent. He grasped the cool, slippery form—a ten inch rainbow!

He took it off the hook and smacked its head against a rock.

"Nice one!"

He startled. A man wearing a fedora and vest and a slick pair of waders stood at the top of the falls. He carried a fly rod.

"What did you catch him on?" the man asked.

Hurley held up his can of corn. The man frowned. "You know this is a fly fishing only stream," he said. "No bait fishing allowed."

The trout slipped out of his hands. He picked it up and dropped it again.

"I didn't see no signs."

"They're posted every 50 yards. That's one right there."

Hurley glanced on the far bank at the small, diamond-shaped sign nailed to the tree. He had seen others, but chose to ignore them.

The man gave him a final hard look, then headed on downstream. Horse's ass. Probably turn him in to the ranger if he came across one.

He stuck the fish in his jacket pocket. The man might wait to see if he kept on fishing, then come back and chew him out again. Best to put some distance between them.

He worked his way upstream, the path reduced to faint smudges of packed earth. Opal might be wondering where he was. Maybe the fisherman would stop and tell her he was just ahead. He pushed his way through a gap in the rhododendron, heard the deep roar of falling water. The gorge was growing narrower and steeper, the creek turning into a series of cascades, each one harder to reach than the last.

He came to a rock outcropping that he couldn't scale. Have to climb the bank. He grabbed a sapling and hauled himself up, his rubber boots slipping on the leaf-littered slope. A wall of rhododendron forced him further up the bank. He moved along the steep slope bracing his feet against whatever roots he could find. The stream grew quiet. That meant deep water.

He sat on his rear end and worked his way down through the rhododendron. He pushed aside the branches and found himself on a steep rock face a dozen feet above the stream. Looked like good water. He edged out onto the mossy rock. Suddenly, the moss gave way. He skidded down, landing hard in the pool, a sharp pain shooting up his right ankle.

It took him a moment to figure out what hurt the most. He'd scraped up his hands and his butt, soaked himself from head to toe. But the ankle was the worst. He tried to take a step, cried out in pain and fell into the frigid water, the current pulling him toward the next drop.

Using his good foot and his free hand, he swam to the far bank and dragged himself onto the rocks. He kicked off his rubber boots and drained out the water. A knob of bone protruded under his sock. Ankle was broke.

"Opal!"

The rushing stream swallowed his cry.

"Opal!

He glanced at the treetops. The light was going fast. She'd be starting to worry. Probably, she would wait until dark, then go back up to the truck. But by then, everyone else would be gone. And he had the keys.

He started to shake. The weatherman had said the temperature was supposed to drop into the 30s. He'd freeze to death if he didn't get covered. He remembered a story one of his Daddy's friends had told about getting lost in the woods during a squirrel hunt—the only way he'd survived the night was by covering himself with leaves.

He rolled onto his hands and knees and pulled himself over the moss-covered rocks. There was a flat spot on dry ground just wide enough for him to lie down. He snugged up against the bank and started pulling down leaves. He covered his boots and pants, and finally his chest.

An odor like old tennis sneakers permeated the air—galax. He searched the ground for the shiny green leaf, but it was already too dark. The canopy above was just a silhouette against the narrow band of sky. Soon, the streamside rhododendrons merged with the rocks, then the tree trunks with the hills.

As he lay with his head on his arm, he heard a sound in the woods. Was that a footstep? Could be a deer, or maybe a bear. There it was again, in a different direction. Something familiar about that. Acorns. It was acorns falling from the trees. And there was another sound, a ticking in the branches. A feathery form landed on his face—a leaf. The leaves were coming down.

The last of the blue bled out of the sky. No one would come now. For the first time in his life, he felt utterly alone. He'd always thought of nature as a friend, but now he knew it didn't care a whit about him. Not him or anyone else. Tears welled in his eyes. God was punishing him for what he'd done—to Opal, to Patsy, to Buddy, to Noah. One by one their faces loomed before him—the abandoned, the shamed, and the dead.

"I'm sorry," he wept. "I'm so sorry."

Chapter 43

Opal awoke looking into the eyes of a fox. Was she dreaming? The creature was so close she could hear it sniffing, black nose inching forward. She tried to touch it, but she couldn't move. Why was she lying on the ground?

A sound of tires on gravel. The fox fled, its long tail held straight out behind.

A door slammed. "Ma'am, are you O.K.?"

She lifted her gaze to see a man in a hat and a fishing vest. He knelt down and touched her forehead. "What happened? Did you fall?"

It was then that she felt the chill all through her body. Her toes and fingers were numb.

"Cold," she said.

The man shed his jacket and put it around her shoulders. "Can you get up?" he said. "I'll help you into my car."

She tried and failed to roll onto her knees. The man let go of her hand and stood back.

"You were with that man, weren't you? Is he your husband?"

She didn't know who he was talking about.

"Is that your truck?" the man said.

She rolled her head to see a red truck just behind her. The man pulled on the door, but it wouldn't open. "You've been here all night, haven't you?"

He looked toward the woods. "Can you tell me your husband's name?"

Husband? She didn't have a husband. She was dating Happy Watson, but they were not married.

The man hollered into the valley. "Hello!"

Another car approached. The man trotted into the road and waved his arms. He talked with the driver. The car turned around and went away.

"He's gone to get help," the man said. "You're going to be alright."

She grew afraid. Something bad had happened. Something had happened and it was her fault. "Momma," she cried. "Momma."

* * *

The gravel crackled again and a big, white truck pulled in. Opal read the lettering on the side—*Watauga County Ambulance Service*. Watauga County. Where was that?

A man and a woman wearing matching jackets stepped out of the cab. They talked briefly with the fishermen, then leaned down to speak to her.

"Ma'am can you tell me how you hurt your head?"

"I don't know."

"Can you repeat that?"

"I don't know."

He barked over his shoulder. "Bring me some blankets. We've got to get her warmed up."

Here came another truck. A fire engine. More people gathered in the parking lot, talking about some man.

"I saw him about half a mile upstream," the fisherman said. "Old guy. Probably in his seventies."

A face leaned overhead. "Ma'am, can you tell us when you last saw your husband?"

"I don't ha a husband," she said.

"I can't understand her," the man said. "Let's get her loaded up."

They rolled her onto a stretcher and put her in the back of the truck. The woman with the heavy jacket climbed in beside her. She stuck a needle in her arm that hooked it up to a bag of clear liquid.

For a long time, she lay looking at the bright lights overhead. Every now and then, the woman would lean over her and ask if she was warm enough.

She shook her head, shivering uncontrollably. The back door opened.

"We've got the husband here."

There was a commotion and in beside her rolled a man on a stretcher, a filthy man, his clothes covered in dirt and smelling of creek mud. He raised his head and spoke through chattering teeth.

"That's Opal," he said.

Who was this man?

"I fell up the stream," he said. "I couldn't get back to you."

She cried out to the woman in the jacket.

"She's a bit confused," the woman said. "Do you recognize your husband, Opal? This is Hurley."

She shook her head.

The woman studied her face. “Has her mouth always hung down on this side?”

“No,” the man said. “Something ain’t right.”

The woman reached behind her in a cabinet and took out some pills. She filled a cup of water.

“I’m going to give you some aspirin,” the woman said.

She lifted her head, put the pills in her mouth, and gave her some water. She swallowed and coughed, spilling water down her neck. She was making a terrible mess.

“We’re ready to roll,” a voice said.

The doors shut and the truck began to move. Maybe they were taking her home. Wherever it was, she prayed they wouldn’t leave her with this awful man.

Chapter 44

Renata sat at the dining table with the cards and letters spread before her. "Here's one from Ann Roby," she said. "Remember her daughter, Katy, was killed in a car accident two years ago? She says she spends some time every morning imagining a conversation with Katy. It helps keep her alive in her mind."

Danny dropped a fork into the dishwasher. "Lovely."

"I don't even know this person. Krista Ford. She says she's a friend of Susie Winkler's. 'I'm so sorry to hear of your son's death. My daughter, Mia, died of brain cancer last year at age 12. Needless to say, it's been the hardest year of my life…' "

"What is this, The Dead Baby Club?"

Renata pushed the letters across the table. "Here, you read them."

Danny got up and stood in front of the sliding glass door and stared out at the falling leaves. "I might go into work this afternoon. I've got a bunch of papers to grade."

"I thought you were going to get the leaves up before Hurley and Opal came back?"

"Yeah fine."

Outside, the cool air filled her nostrils. Noah would be with her now, anytime she used the leaf blower. He would run ahead of her to the car shed and grab the handle of the machine, excited that his Mom could use something so loud and strong.

She retrieved the blower from the garage and pulled the starter chord. The leaves lay in a thick carpet on their side of the drive. She swept the blower side to side, driving them toward the yard. With each pass, the wall of leaves grew thicker. The column slowed and then stopped altogether, the blower too weak to budge them another inch. She shut it off, went back to the car shed and got a rake.

Standing at one end of the row, she swatted at the leaves, moving the pile a yard toward the woods. She moved a yard and swatted the pile another yard. Within half-an-hour, she was exhausted. The pile lay midway across the lawn like a giant snake. Fuck this.

She went back inside, found the family room empty. Renata had left the cards scattered on the table. She should have been kinder to her about those. People were just trying to help. She went down the hall and found Renata sitting on the floor in front of the closet.

"What are you doing?"

Renata covered her hand. "Nothing."

"Is that a rosary?"

"Yes."

She sat beside her and put her arm around her shoulder. "Renata. Come on. You don't need that hocus pocus."

She pushed him away. "You smell like gasoline."

"Yeah, O.K."

Danny went into the bathroom and ran the shower. It might not do any good, but she was going to deny Renata any excuse.

She scrubbed herself down with Dr. Bronner's peppermint soap and shampooed her hair. She stood before the mirror toweling herself off. She'd lost weight since Noah's death.

Depression did wonders for curbing your appetite. She wrapped the towel around her chest and came into the bedroom. Renata sat on the bed reading. She had put the rosary away.

"How do I smell now?"

Renata smiled. "Better."

She let the towel drop and eased herself onto the bed.

"What are you doing?" Renata said.

"What do you think?"

She lowered herself onto Renata and kissed her, slowly, softly.

"Please," she breathed. "I need you."

She undid the buttons of Renata's shirt, unsnapped her bra. She kissed her nipples, slid down her belly and pulled off her pants and panties. She reached her arms under Renata's knees and parted her legs to reveal her dark bush. The passion that had been bottled up for so long began to flow. She wanted to devour Renata's clit, make her moan. Instead, Renata pushed her away.

"What?"

"I can't."

"You're kidding?"

Renata rolled onto her side and drew her knees to her chest. "I'm sorry. I can't stop thinking about him."

She sat up and held her head in her hands. This couldn't be happening. "I know what it is," she said. "You don't want me."

Chapter 45

Hurley rose up on his crutches and made his way down the carpeted hall into Buddy and Leanne's kitchen. Leanne stood at the sink under the bright glow of the recessed lights.

"Good morning, Hurley. Did you sleep well?"

The meanness was gone from her voice. Moving into this house had done her good.

He leaned his crutches against the counter and sat at the table. "I never slept in a queen bed before. It's right comfortable."

"Can I get you something?"

"Whatever you're having."

She poured a cup of tea and set it down in front of him. "Give that bag a couple of minutes," she said.

He bounced the tea bag up and down. "Buddy gone to work?"

"If you can call it that. Mostly they just sit around the trailer. They haven't had a serious job in a couple of months. If it wasn't for Duke Hospital, they'd be out of business."

She sat at the table and looked him in the eye. "Are you up for visiting Opal today?"

"I expect so."

"Let me warn you, a stroke changes everything. When Daddy had his, the whole marriage changed."

"I just want to get her home."

"You may wish she was back in the hospital with everything you'll have to do for her, especially with your bad leg. My advice to you is to get someone to help you, at least until you get off those crutches."

"I don't need help."

Leanne gave him a snippy look. "How are you going to bathe her? She may not even be able to dress herself."

He had no answer.

"She may recover some, but don't expect her to be like she was. The doctors told us that's not going to happen."

He knew what the doctors had said, but he didn't believe it. Maybe Opal was just confused after hitting her head. People took time to recover.

"I appreciate all you and Buddy are doing," he said. "Taking me in."

Leanne's smile was sincere. "Well, you're family."

* * *

Eight stories straight up and wide as a football field, Duke Hospital was the largest building he'd ever seen. As he and Leanne waited for Buddy to park the car, an endless parade of people streamed past. Where did they all come from? How could he have lived in this town for 70 years and not know a one of them?

"I'm going inside to get Opal some flowers," Leanne said. "Do you want to wait out here?"

He nodded. There was so much to see, it was like a miniature city. As he stared up at the glass tower, the air reverberated with the whop of rotor blades. A helicopter appeared above the tree line, slowed and dropped behind the building. He'd seen many one of these medevac choppers pass over the farm, but never knew exactly where they landed. The victim must be badly hurt. Maybe a car wreck or a shooting.

Buddy arrived and together they walked through the automatic doors. "Did you see that helicopter?" Hurley said.

Buddy nodded. "They come and go here all day."

"First time I've seen one land."

The sounds of the outdoors faded as they turned down this hallway and that. Leanne followed the color coded letters, but soon became lost.

"They said to turn left at the elevators, but there's elevators here and another set over there," she said.

A passing doctor helped them on their way. Finally, they found the nurse's station for the clinic.

The head nurse, Irene Booker, introduced herself to the family and told them she had Opal all set up. She led the way down the hall and opened the door of Room 105.

On the bed nearest the door lay a tiny, shriveled head, lost in a sea of white. He didn't believe it was Opal. Maybe she was the one behind the curtain.

"Hey, Ma. How are you feeling?" Buddy leaned in and kissed her.

Opal turned to reveal the bandage on her forehead. A frail voice said, "I can't s'eak."

"That's alright. We can understand you."

Buddy got him a chair so he could sit in close. He leaned his crutches against the wall and put on a smile. "How you feeling, Opal? You didn't recognize me when I was in that ambulance."

"At was luh-ee."

He turned to Ms. Booker. "Wha'd she say?"

"She said, 'That was lucky.' She hasn't lost her sense of humor."

He smiled. Opal had never said that kind of thing before. He picked up her arm and rubbed it as if priming a pump.

Leanne held up the flowers. "Look what I brought you, Opal. I'm going to set these in a vase beside the bed."

There was a knock on the door and a man in a white coat stepped in. He introduced himself as Doctor Klein, shaking hands all around before turning to Opal. "How are we doing today, Mrs. Cates?"

Her gaze followed him as he checked her pulse.

"She's having some trouble speaking," Ms. Booker said.

The doctor nodded. "She seems to have lost control on the right side of her body. It makes it difficult for her to pronounce some words. I'm more concerned about her eating. We've got her on an IV and she's swallowed some liquids, but she needs to start taking some solid food."

Hurley frowned. "She can't come home yet?"

"No, she's going to be here awhile. Don't worry. She's in good company."

Leanne patted his shoulder, said something about this being the best place for now, but he could only fight back the tears. Opal was not coming home.

Ms. Booker excused herself, saying she'd be in the office if they had any questions. He glanced at the curtain that sealed off the other bed.

"That's Mrs. Albright," the doctor said. "She and Opal have become friends." He called through the curtain. "Would you like to meet the Cates family?

A cheery voice answered. "That'd be alright."

The doctor drew the curtain back. A colored woman! Broad black face. Salt and pepper hair. She glanced around the room, smiled at him and Buddy. "I can see these two are related," she said.

Buddy smiled. "He's my Pa."

"Your momma and I are getting' to be good friends, aren't we, Ms. Cates?"

He tugged on Buddy's sleeve. "Help me up."

"Do you need to go to the bathroom?"

He grabbed his crutches, swung out of the room and down the hall.

Ms. Booker was sitting at her desk.

"What do you mean putting Opal in with colored?" he said.

"I beg your pardon?"

"You heard me."

"For one thing, Mr. Cates, we aren't allowed to discriminate by race," she said. "For another, that was the only bed available. I find Mrs. Albright a delightful woman. Has Opal voiced some objection?"

"You know she can't say nothing close as she is."

Ms. Booker frowned. "If it becomes clear they can't get along, we will look for something else. But we won't move her based on your concern."

"We'll see about that." He swung back down the hall and into Opal's room. The doctor was gone. He was going to have to speak to Opal directly.

"Pull that curtain closed," he said to Buddy. "I need to ask you and Leanne to leave. I want to speak to Opal in private."

When Buddy and Leanne had gone, he spoke low to Opal. "I'm gonna get you moved to another room."

"Ut?"

"I'll get you in with white."

She waved her hand and looked away.

"I know you blame me for leaving you by the stream," he said. "I'm not leaving you now. Not in here."

"I own wa move."

"I can't understand what you're saying."

Mrs. Albright's voice rang out. "She say, 'She don't want to move.' "

Chapter 46

Two weeks after returning from the mountains, Hurley took his first visit back to the house. Buddy dropped him at the top of the drive and headed off to do some chores. As the backfires of the truck faded in the distance, he took in his surroundings. Renata and Danny's cars were gone. At least he wouldn't have to deal with them. Gus came out from under his bush and approached on stiff legs. He leaned forward and rubbed the top of the dog's head. "Hey, boy. We're a mess, ain't we?"

He glanced at Danny and Renata's back yard. Someone had raked the leaves halfway to the woods and stopped. The two stumps were still there, one tilted toward the sky, the other pulled all the way over by his tractor and chain. They'd found Noah's mud-caked body underneath.

He wiped away tears and turned to study his own yard, covered with leaves around the house. It would take days of raking to get them up. He couldn't even think of doing that until he got off his crutches. Gutters needed cleaning, too.

The thought of entering the empty house scared him, so he headed out to the toolshed to see if anything had been stolen. It didn't take long for people to recognize when a place was empty.

A newspaper left to sit out by the road, leaves in the yard—all kinds of signs for those that were looking.

Finding that all the tools as he left them, he moved on to the vegetable garden. That was a sorry mess. Tomato plants stood dead in their cages. The collards and okra were overgrown. Gus sniffed among the plants, then turned, waiting for him to make the next move.

It took some navigation, but he managed to hold open the storm door and let himself into the kitchen. He switched on the light and stepped inside. The smell of Pine Sol reminded him that Opal had scrubbed the counters just before they left. He opened the refrigerator and sniffed the carton of milk. That would have to be thrown out. Maybe the eggs. He didn't know.

He went into the bedroom and stood for a time. Would Opal be able to get in and out of that bed? Would she need help opening the dresser? Her suitcase stood by the closet where Dwayne had left it. He leaned one of his crutches against the wall and swung the suitcase onto the bed. He unsnapped the latches and studied the neatly folded clothes. The dress Opal had worn at the Daniel Boone lay on top. He took that out and set it to one side. He held up a bra. How could you tell if a bra needed washing? It didn't seem to be dirty, so he set it on top of the dress. Panties. He held them up to the light, saw they were soiled. A man ought not to look at such things. He set that to the other side of the suitcase.

When he was through sorting Opal's clothes, he got a paper bag out of the kitchen and put the dirty clothes inside. He'd take those back for Leanne to launder. He walked out into the living room, opened the front door and stepped onto the porch.

The view was different with half the forked oak gone. Everything seemed out of balance—the tree with its ugly scar, branches all grown to one side. He looked out over the valley for awhile, watched the cars pass on the road. Did any of them know his life had been turned upside down? Did any of them care? The season's last crickets chirped a faint tune, some continuous, some pulsing like a heartbeat—on, off, on, off, on, off.

A car slowed and turned in the drive. Here came Danny. He hadn't spoken to either of them since the service. She got out of the car, dark circles under her eyes like a picture of death.

She spoke without enthusiasm "Look who's here."

He worked his way down the steps and met her at the edge of the drive. "How you been?"

"About like you'd expect."

There wasn't anything more to say.

"Leanne told us about Opal's stroke," she said. "That's bad news."

"They got her in rehab over at Duke. She can't hardly move the right side of her body. Don't speak too good."

"Do you get over to see her often?"

"Every day. They got her in with a colored woman."

"Oh, yeah? How's that going?"

"They're getting to be friends. Nurse says she's the only one can make Opal smile."

"That's nice."

He was gladdened by Danny's response. Maybe she could tell he'd changed. "I guess you heard I fell off a rock. Spent the night laying out in the woods."

"Yes, I did. You must have been terrified."

"Rescue squad come and got me. If I'd laid out there another night, I'd be dead."

Danny shook her head. "How long are you going to be on crutches?"

"Doctor said another two weeks. I'm staying with Buddy and Leanne."

"That's great that they took you in."

"They're family."

A car turned up the drive. Renata. He felt a mixture of dread and hope. Maybe she'd be sympathetic knowing all he'd been through. Probably not.

She stepped out of the car with a bag of groceries. Even from a distance, she looked awful. Her cheeks were splotched with red. Her eyes were watery, haunted.

She greeted him with a non-committal hello.

"I come back for a look around."

She looked at his crutches. "Buddy said you broke your ankle."

"I took a bad fall."

She offered no expression of sympathy.

"How's Opal?"

"She's in rehab. Be a couple of weeks before she can come home."

"We miss seeing her."

He nodded in appreciation, but her words tore him up. She didn't miss him. Didn't want to see him now, maybe ever.

"I need to get these groceries inside."

Danny lingered in the drive. "I'm sorry Renata's not being very communicative," she said.

"Does she blame me for what happened?"

"She blames everybody."

He winced.

"Well, I better get inside," she said. "It's good to see you. Give my best to Opal."

Chapter 47

Hurley walked alone down the hospital corridor, familiar now with the building and its receptionists. He knocked on the half-opened door. From her bed, Mrs. Albright beckoned him in.

He set his crutches against the wall. "Mind if I set awhile?"

"No," she said. "You can pull that curtain closed if you want."

"That's alright."

He sat in the chair and stared down the length of the bed. Opal lay on her back with her mouth open.

"Is she asleep?" he asked.

"I expect so. She hasn't moved in awhile. Why don't you bring your chair over here where she can see you better?"

He slid the chair between the two beds, his back to Mrs. Albright. Opal looked a hundred years old, her face and hands spotted and wrinkled.

"How's she been?" he said.

"She was right perky this morning. Pulled that IV tube out. She doesn't care for it at all."

"Maybe she was just bothered."

"The nurse put it back in and told her not to fuss with it. Opal gave her a look."

He smiled. "I know that look."

Mrs. Albright pointed at the newspaper. "What did you bring her?"

"I'd guess you'd call it a flower." He unfolded the paper to reveal a thin branch with spear-shaped leaves and clusters of pink nuts and bright red centers.

"It's what they call 'Hearts A'Bustin.' Grows wild along my fence line. Most of the time, it don't look like nothing. Right now is when it opens up."

"I declare."

"I thought maybe they'd have a jar I could set it in, give it some water."

"Might not last any longer with water. Wild flowers are like that."

He laid the branch on the bedside table. Opal was sleeping soundly. He turned to Mrs. Albright. "What do they have you in for?"

"Diabetes. I done lost my leg."

She pulled her sheet back to reveal a stump below the knee.

"Diabetes done that to you?"

"I got bad circulation. Don't know what they'll take next. Probably my head."

He ran his hand across Opal's forehead. She stirred, opened her eyes.

"Opal. I brought you something." He held the branch. "It come from out by the garden."

She looked uncertainly at the branch. "Poo over there," she said.

He set the branch on the shelf. "She don't care about flowers."

Mrs. Albright raised her head. "Come on, now, Mrs. Cates, you can smile."

She and Opal locked eyes. Opal brightened.

"There it is," Mrs. Albright said. "Smiles like a little girl, don't she?"

He nodded. "It's for you."

"It's for you, too."

"Naw. She ain't smiling at me. She's mad at me."

"Why would she be mad at you?"

"I left her back at the creek. If I'd a stayed with her, she might not have had that stroke."

"You don't know that."

He stroked her forehead. She looked at him again. "Is Passy coming?"

"Patsy? No, Patsy ain't coming."

Opal's eyes lost focus. She rolled away from him.

"Who's she talking about?" Mrs. Albright asked.

"Patsy's our daughter. She died a while back."

Mrs. Albright sighed. "I'm sorry. People get that way when they've had a stroke. Asking for relatives that have passed."

"It's the ones they want to see most, I expect."

Mrs. Alright smiled. "She'll see her by and by."

He looked at the colored woman. "You believe in heaven?"

"Yes, I do."

"There's some don't believe in either one."

"I know what my Bible says."

Her words were a comfort. He was sorry he'd insulted her by trying to get Opal moved. He couldn't bring himself to apologize, but he was pretty sure she knew how he felt. That ought to be enough.

* * *

The day after Thanksgiving, Opal came home. He and Buddy lifted her from the truck into the wheelchair, and pointed her towards the new ramp that crossed the patio to the back door.

"You see what Buddy and I done?"

"At's nice."

Buddy held the storm door open and Hurley wheeled Opal into the kitchen. He paused to let her take it in. "You're back now," he beamed.

She glanced around the kitchen. "How I gaw reach the ca'nets?"

"You ain't until you can stand."

He wheeled her up to the table, while Buddy helped her off with her coat. "I'm gonna take care of the meals," he said.

"Wha' you been making?"

"I'm pretty good at spaghetti. Leanne taught me."

Opal motioned toward the refrigerator. "Lemme see."

He opened the door to reveal a carton of milk, butter, and eggs.

"I need you to help nake a list," Opal said.

"Do you want to see what we done in the bedroom?" Buddy asked.

He wheeled her into Patsy's old room where the rented hospital bed stood.

"You got a whole room to yourself," he said.

"'At's nice."

"We took the door off the bathroom in the hall so you can get in and out in the wheelchair," Hurley said.

Opal looked down the hall. "Folk's gaw see me."

"We ain't gonna be entertaining," he said.

They wheeled her back into the kitchen, where he presented the grocery bag full of mail. "Look at all this," he said. "There's lots that care about you."

Opal lifted a letter with her good hand, stared at the return address.

"We opened 'em for you, but we ain't read 'em," Buddy said.

For the rest of the afternoon, Opal sat at the kitchen table and read the letters. Hurley could tell by her eyes how she appreciated them.

"'Is one's from Danny and Rena-a," she said. "Ha' you talked to them?"

"I did once. Danny seemed alright. Renata didn't have much to say."

Opal sighed, put the letter down. "How I gonna answer these? I can har'ly write."

"People ain't expecting you to write back. You can tell 'em when you see 'em."

He moved to the stove. "You gettin' hungry?"

"I guess."

"I thought we'd have spaghetti tonight."

Opal watched as he brought out the jars of tomatoes and tomato sauce. He carefully browned the ground beef and poured the contents together.

"You gonna drain the fat?" she asked.

He looked up. "Am I supposed to do that?"

After dinner, he helped Opal into the bathroom and onto the toilet. He made a point of going back to the kitchen, rattling the pots and pans until he heard the toilet flush. He helped her into her nightgown and, finally, into bed. "You need me just knock on the wall." He kissed her on the forehead. "Everything's gonna be alright."

Chapter 48

In the morning, Hurley helped Opal dress. She was able to use her one good hand to put on her underwear, but could not manage her bra and refused his help.

"L'em hang," she said.

He made her a "special" breakfast of bacon and eggs. Eager to show her he could cook more than spaghetti, he was hurt to see her struggle to pick a piece of shell out of her teeth. Everything he did fell short somehow.

Opal struggled, too. She wanted to get back to knitting the sweater that she'd been making for L. Dog, but couldn't hold the needles steady in her right hand. He suggested she wedge her right arm against the chair. After a few failed attempts, she managed to wrap the yarn over that needle and push the other needle through. She completed a second stitch and a third.

"Now, you're getting' it," he said. "Mind if I go down and get the paper?"

"Go'ne."

Outside a steady drizzle cloaked the hill in a gray mist. Even with that, it felt good to be outside. He strode down the drive, feeling the freedom of not having to care for an invalid.

It was the day after Thanksgiving, the busiest shopping day of the year. Down on Hope Valley Road, a steady progression of cars whooshed past. Opal would be sad to know she was missing the chance to hunt for bargains. Maybe she could do that at some point in the future, but he would have to go with her, help her in and out of the truck. It dawned on him that any time she wanted to go anywhere—to the grocery store, the beauty parlor, to church, to the doctor—he was going to have to take her.

He picked up the paper and headed back to the house, looking forward to seeing how far Opal had gotten with her knitting, but when he came through the door, he found her in tears.

"I drot the yarn."

He spied the ball of yarn under the coffee table. "Let me get it for you."

"I called and called."

He set it back on her lap. "How 'bout I put you on the couch? You can set sideways and hold the yarn against the back with your leg."

He took her arm and lifted her to a standing position. She took a step with her good leg, dragged her other foot across the carpet and collapsed forward onto the couch. He turned her around and stretched her bad leg out. He wedged the yarn between her thigh and the couch back and handed her the knitting.

"You alright, now?"

"I reckon."

* * *

By mid-afternoon, Hurley was itching to get out again. He usually went to Taylor's Exxon around noon to get a Coke and chat with Russell, but first he had to feed Opal, then put her down for a nap.

She frowned as he helped her undress. “You snell li’ an old dog. When’s the last tine you did a wash?”

“It’s been awhile.” He didn’t want to admit that he’d not done a wash since her stroke. “I’ll do it directly.”

Once he’d tucked Opal in bed, he stripped down to his briefs and carried the clothes basket to the laundry. He peered into the washer. Which went first, the clothes or the detergent? He read the label on the box. “Put clothes in washer and add detergent.” Did you put it in all at once or a little at a time?

He stuck his head in the bedroom. Opal was asleep. Guessing the detergent would not mix well if smothered with clothes, he poured some powder into the washer, added a layer of clothes, then sprinkled in more. After doing that with several layers, he closed the door and eyed the wash settings—Delicates, Whites, Colors, Normal. Which were these? The clothes had Color, but they might be Normal, too. He decided on Normal.

As the washer ran through its cycles, he sat in the kitchen and tried to read the paper. He glanced out the window. The rain had stopped. He really wanted to get over to Taylor’s. Finally, the washer fell silent. He switched the clothes over to the dryer, and went out on the front porch. The light was getting on toward late afternoon. Cars were coming back from the mall.

Tired of waiting for the dryer’s buzzer, he opened the door and pulled out his work shirt and pants. A little damp. Not too bad. He slipped them on and peeked in on Opal. Still asleep. He hurried out to the truck and sped down the drive.

Russell looked up as he came through the door, his burly hands holding a stack of bills. “You get caught in a snowstorm?”

“What you talking ‘bout?”

"You got white stuff all over your clothes."

He looked at his pants, brushed the powder away. "Washer ain't working right."

Russell smiled. "I'll bet."

He took a seat by the drink machine. "Mind if I have one?"

"Do I ever?" Russell studied the newspaper. "Y'all have a nice Thanksgiving?"

"We got Opal back home."

"How's she doing?"

"I've got to do everything for her. Dress her, cook dinner."

"Do the laundry."

He frowned. "First time I've been out all day 'cept to get the paper."

"I'm sure she appreciates your taking all that on."

"If I do something wrong, she snaps at me."

Russell sighed. "They say there's nothing like a stroke to turn a marriage upside down."

He picked up a fishing magazine off the counter and studied the cover, a picture of a man holding up a giant mackerel. Normally, he'd spend fifteen minutes leafing through the magazine, but the thought of Opal waking alone stopped him. He set it back on the counter.

"I better get on back."

"You're a good man, Hurley."

Chapter 49

New Years Day, alone in his house, Marvin blew his head off with his shotgun. Hurley saw the police car and ambulance in the driveway. He didn't tell Opal, saying only that he was going out for a walk.

He approached a policeman outside the door and introduced himself as a neighbor and friend. The policeman asked if he knew of any family members they could contact.

"He's got a sister in Fayetteville. Her address might be somewhere inside."

The door opened and an EMT wheeled Marvin's body out covered in a blanket.

"Last thing, sir," the policeman said. "I would ask you if you could help us make a positive ID on the body. His face is pretty well shot off, but maybe you could use something else."

He approached the gurney. "Lemme see his hands."

The EMT lifted the blanket. He studied the age spots. "That's him."

Back in the house, Opal asked what he saw on his walk.

"I picked up some trash down by the road. You ready to take your bath?"

He ran the tub and helped Opal out of her clothes. Nothing showed the ravages of time like an old woman's body. She'd been a beauty once with small, lovely breasts and a shapely bottom. Now, she stood hunched over, her breasts hanging like mudflaps, her shoulderblades protruding like a pair of broken wings. He eased her down into the tub.

"Is that too hot?"

"Feels good."

"I'll do your back."

He picked up the washcloth and rubbed it across her neck and shoulders.

"Get iy ears," she said.

He handed her the cloth so she could do her front.

After toweling Opal dry, he helped her into her nightgown and into bed. He leaned over to kiss her forehead.

"Cuh lie with ee," she said.

"You want me to get under the covers?"

He took off his shoes, climbed into bed, and snugged up to her backside. She took his arm and drew it tight to her waist.

"I ready to go to Jesus," she said.

The words ripped his heart out, but he held his composure. "You've got plenty of time."

He pushed his face against her brittle curls, tears welling in his eyes. He loved her more as a cripple than he'd ever loved her healthy.

"I worry about Buh'y. Leanne'll leave if he doesn't 'ake suh 'oney."

"I'll take care of him."

Opal rolled her head back. "You can't baby hin. You got to trea' hin like a 'an."

* * *

When it warmed up in the spring, he wheeled Opal out onto the porch. She liked to watch the cars pass on the road, though they didn't know most of the drivers these days. Every now and again, he'd say, "there goes so and so." Opal would smile and nod. At those times, it was almost possible to believe their lives hadn't changed. But then she would fail to respond and he'd look over to see that she'd fallen asleep.

On the afternoon of April 15, Bradley passed in his UPS truck, his bare legs visible through the open door.

"He's already wearing his short shorts," Hurley said. That always made Opal laugh, but when he looked over, her head fallen to the side. A line of drool ran down her chin.

"Opal."

He got out of his chair and prodded her arm.

"You asleep?"

He put the back of his hand under her nose.

"Opal?"

He pulled his chair close, held her hand, and began to sob. Through his tears, he looked out across the valley. Everything was going to pass—the farm, the big oaks, all the people driving by.

Some time later, Renata came up the drive. She usually avoided his gaze, but this time she stared wide-eyed. She stopped the car in front of the house and got out.

"Is something wrong with Opal?" she asked.

He looked at her, unable to speak.

She climbed the steps and touched the back of her hand to Opal's cheek. "Oh, My God."

"She passed a couple hours ago," he said.

Renata wrapped her arms around him. "Hurley, I'm so sorry." The smell of her skin, sweaty and warm, filled him with gratitude and longing.

"We ought to cover her up," she said.

"I got a blanket on the bed."

"Would you like me to get it?"

"I'll get it."

He'd done some hard things in his life, but there was nothing worse than laying a blanket over Opal. It was degrading, ghostly, the way it took the form of her face. He expected her to reach up and pull it off. But, no, she was dead.

Chapter 50

In the back of his mind, Hurley always held out the notion that he could survive on his own. But in the weeks following Opal's death, loneliness ran through him like a spear. He felt it when he came out in the morning and sat alone at the kitchen table with his bowl of cereal and cup of instant coffee. It hung through him as he rode the John Deere up and down the lawn, his shoulders hunched forward over the wheel. It hit him each time he came in the house and was greeted by silence. Nights he slept alone, as he had since Opal's stroke, but he always knew she was right next door. Now, Patsy's room was empty again.

The first week in May, he was in the kitchen making lunch when he saw Renata's Volkswagon roll up the drive. It wasn't usual for her to come home on a work day, and momentarily, he saw the reason why. A fellow got out of the car with her. Through the open window, he could hear their happy talk. They went inside for awhile then came out on the deck and propped their feet up on the rail.

He went back to making his sandwich, but the bursts of laughter from across the way sent him to the window again.

These two were acting like they were more than just friends. Did Danny know about this?

After a time, the voices went quiet. He looked out the window, but they'd gone inside. The minutes passed—ten, fifteen. Finally, they came out. More laughter, the closing of car doors. They drove off, leaving him with a sick feeling and no one to tell it to.

A few days later, he was out mowing the lawn when Linwood Jernigan pulled into Marvin's drive. He waved, opened the tail gate, and took out a For Sale sign. Hurley finished mowing and settled on the porch with his Red Man, waiting for Linwood to come up the drive.

"Hey, neighbor!" Mind if I pay you a visit?"

Hurley waved him over. The realtor parked his shiny, black SUV and came across the lawn.

"Have a seat."

Linwood put on a serious face. "I sure was sorry to hear about Opal. She was a fine woman."

"We'd have been married 60 years come June."

"That's a lifetime. How've you been doing? Buddy been by to see you?"

"He comes by pretty regular."

"Construction is really picking up now that the interest rates have come down. I imagine he's busy."

"He's working some."

Linwood pointed across the street. "I guess you saw me putting up the sign."

"The sister didn't want the place?"

"Not for what they're asking."

"How much is that?"

"A million and a-half."

He spat. "Ain't no one gonna pay that kind of money for a run-down old farm."

"It's not likely to be a farm. Likely to be a whole other animal."

"You talking 'bout a subdivision? That's bottomland there. It don't even perc."

"I guess you haven't heard. The city's planning on running water and sewer all the way down Hope Valley Road. Gonna happen this summer."

"We ain't in the city."

"We're in the ETJ."

"What you talking about?"

"Extra Territorial Jurisdiction. It's where the city plans to expand. I'm not at liberty to give out the details, but a developer out of Charlotte is talking about putting in a mixed-use development —a thousand homes, club house, tennis courts, swimming pool…"

"On 300 acres?"

"Quarter-acre lots. Of course, they'll have to rezone the land, and that'll involve a public hearing."

He scowled. "They'll damn sure hear from me. I don't want a thousand homes down there. I can't hardly get out in the morning as it is."

Linwood leaned in close. "Here's the thing. I've told the developer I can smooth things out with a certain neighbor if they'll take my advice on hiring a local grading company. Buddy'd do all the roads, the playing fields, the tennis courts…a good year's worth of work. And a who-o-ole lot of money."

Linwood smiled, letting him absorb the message. "Of course, if the neighbor speaks out against it…"

"I ain't gonna say nothing."

"That's good." Linwood leaned back in his seat. "You know you could get a good price for this land once the sewer goes in. You could even do a like-kind-exchange, get yourself 40 acres and a nice house somewhere further out and not spend a dime in capital gains."

"I told you before, I ain't moving."

"O.K. I hear you." Linwood looked across the drive. "How are your neighbors doing? I hear they've had a hard time since their boy got killed."

"Where'd you hear that?"

"Word gets around." Linwood shook his head. "It'd be hard on any couple. Tragedy like that. Sometimes the best thing to do is go your separate ways and start over."

* * *

He waited for a sign from the neighbors—doors slamming, screaming, someone moving out. But all remained quiet. She brought the man back again for "lunch." This time, Hurley made a point of being seen, walking back to the car shed while they were out on the deck. Their voices fell silent, but they made no move to leave.

Now, more than ever, he felt the hill divided. He stayed to his side of the driveway, the women to theirs. If any of them happened to be outside at the same time or pass each other on the drive, he or she might offer a polite wave, sometimes not even that. Danny was friendlier than Renata, but even she was restrained.

So he was surprised one morning working in the front garden to see Danny come across the lawn. She was in no hurry, gazing at the sky, her hands in the pockets of her sweatshirt.

"Hey, there," she said. "What are you planting?"

Her voice seemed relaxed. Maybe she didn't know about Renata. Or maybe they worked it out.

"Limas. Snap beans. I like some for later in the summer."

"I see the tomatoes are coming in. Did you plant any cherry tomatoes?"

"You know I don't like cherries."

"I thought maybe things had changed."

He ran the hoe back and forth through the soil. "I didn't plant anything out back this year. I guess you know that."

"Yeah, we didn't do anything either."

He decided to risk an invitation. They'd gotten to know each other gardening. Maybe they could come together again. "Not too late to plant a few things," he said. "You're welcome to use these rows here. I don't need any more beans."

"Seriously?"

"You might not like me spraying the weeds."

"Maybe you should try something different."

He smiled. "I'm too old for that."

Danny watched him. "I read about this huge development they're planning for Marvin's land. That's terrible."

"Something, ain't it?"

"Can you imagine a thousand homes over there? It just wouldn't be the same."

"Nope."

"You don't seem very concerned."

The truth was he didn't know what to feel. With Opal gone, Noah dead, Renata hardly speaking to him, the hill seemed cursed. He'd been mulling over Linwood's offer, and it was starting to make sense. He'd made a mess of his life, but maybe he could do something for Buddy.

"The article said the city will have to rezone the land, so there'll be a public hearing," she said. "We could speak out against it. I certainly plan to. And you've lived here longer than anyone in the area. People will listen to you."

He stopped hoeing. "So you ain't planning to move?"

"No." She eyed him suspiciously. "Listen, I'm sorry we haven't been better neighbors lately. It's been really hard. Renata's grown pretty distant. It's not just you she's shutting out."

He nodded. "Did she tell you about the fella she's had over?"

"What fellow?"

"I don't know him. They've come a couple of times for lunch. I've seem them out on the deck."

"Tall guy with brown curly hair?"

"That's him."

"Shit. James."

"I thought you ought to know about it."

She shook her head. "This changes everything."

Chapter 51

"Did you fuck him?"

Danny stood at the entrance to the kitchen, Renata at the sink.

"No. He just came over for lunch."

"More than once, according to Hurley. Turn around and look at me. Did you fuck him?"

Renata covered her face with her hands as the tears began to flow. "Yes."

She exploded. "God! I can't believe it. How long were you going to hide this from me?"

"I'm so sorry," Renata said. "I'm so so sorry."

She shook her head in disgust. "What is it? Do you love him or do you just want some dick? I know you've wanted James' dick."

"I don't know," Renata said.

"Of course I don't count to him. I'm just your lesbian lover. We're not even married."

"He likes you, actually."

"Oh, please." She glared at Renata. "Do you even like me? I know you blame me for Noah. That's pretty obvious."

"I don't know. I just want to feel good."

"Oh, yeah? How do you feel now?"

"Terrible."

Seeing Renata cower in the corner, she couldn't believe how the woman she'd loved had become so ugly. Her mouth was stretched like a chimpanzee's, her lying eyes desperate and afraid.

"You know it galls me," she said. "All the rules you set for yourself, all the precautions. Be careful of this. Don't let Noah do that. And then you go and do something incredibly reckless that ends up destroying our whole relationship."

Renata flushed bright red, her face knotted with rage. "Me, reckless? You've always said 'let Noah do this, let Noah do that. How's he ever going to grow up to be a man if he can't ride around on the lawn mower?' Well, he'll never get the chance to grow up because of your recklessness. Yours and Hurley's."

She shook her head. "So what do you want me to do? Do you want me to stay or go?"

"I don't know."

"Fine. I'm leaving. You can fuck James all you want."

Chapter 52

As he turned the truck onto the new Interstate, Hurley's spirits lifted. He was leaving, heading for the coast. Big green exit signs boasted the names of families—Davis, Hopkins, Page—-whom Hurley had once known, simple farmers living on dirt roads bearing their names. Now, these roads were paved and lined with office buildings. Everything in the Triangle was changing.

The interstate circled around Raleigh, fancy new office towers looming on the horizon. Then it turned back to two lanes, sloping down to the coastal plain and on through flat farm country. The fields used to shine with the yellow-green of bright leaf tobacco, but since the government came out against smoking, it was all soybeans and cotton.

Somewhere near Clinton, he caught a stench like ammonia. Through the trees, he glimpsed one of the new-fangled hog barns, where a thousand pigs stood on cement grates that carried their shit into an outdoor lagoon. You could smell that for miles when the wind was right.

The coast came abruptly. One minute, you were driving through a pine plantation, the next you were at the water's edge, ship masts crossing back and forth beneath the raised bridge. He turned down the sand road that led down to the trailer park. Harris was sitting out by the waterway. He gave Hurley a wave and a sympathetic smile. He knew about Opal.

He unlocked the trailer and turned on the air conditioner. Right away, he noticed the soft spot on the floor. He put his weight on it, saw discoloration on the linoleum. Water must have come up this far during the hurricane. The subfloor would have to be replaced.

He went into the bedroom and sat his suitcase on the bed. Opal's watercolor lay on the side table. He smiled thinking how much she enjoyed making that shell frame. He leaned it against the table lamp and opened the sliding glass doors.

"Come on down here," Harris called. "Bugs need to pick on someone besides me."

He crossed the sand road and sat beside Harris. "My linoleum's buckled up," he said. "How'd you make out?"

"I already had mine replaced," Harris said. "It's no problem. Insurance'll cover it."

They looked out at the water.

"I'm sorry to hear about Opal," Harris said. "She was a decent woman."

"Appreciate it," he said.

"Hell, I ain't been no good to anyone since Mattie passed. I just come down here to sweep out the dust."

A cabin cruiser passed on the waterway, a sun-tanned man and woman steering from the flying bridge.

"That's the good life there," Hurley said.

Harris shook his head. "You don't know for sure what anyone's feeling. I seen a couple come off one of those boats over at Blalock's. They set down for dinner next to me and Hattie, neither one of them said a word the whole time."

Harris was right. You couldn't tell what was going on in anyone's head. There were lonely people everywhere.

"Do you want to get dinner?" he said. "Me and Opal liked to go to the Fish House."

"I like Dirty Dicks, but I'll go to the Fish House."

They drove over the bridge to the restaurant and took a seat by the window. At first, Hurley was glad to have company, but it didn't take long for the mood to sour.

"I didn't ask for cole slaw," Harris told the waitress when she brought his catfish.

Opal never would have been so rude to a waitress. He tried to brighten the mood by talking about the Tarheels, but Harris dismissed him.

"I don't pay attention to football."

He realized how impossible it was to find someone you could tolerate for more than a few hours. No one could ever replace Opal.

Back in the trailer, he sat on the bed and cradled Opal's watercolor. Tears welled forth as he ran his fingers over the shell frame. These silly pastimes were what made up a life.

At sunrise, he drove out to the beach and parked at the pier house. He walked over the dune and stood before the ocean. It was a calm morning, sun glinting off the surface. Opal liked to come early to hunt for shells before they got picked over. Already, people were out looking, heads bent to the ground. There'd be shell frames for every house.

He struggled in his high-topped leather shoes through the soft sand above the tide line. When he reached the hard pack by the water he headed north away from the sun. The waves broke low and smooth, white foam sliding before him and melting into the sand. Children were already out playing in the puddles left by the tide. Their mommas called from under their umbrellas. "You be careful, Aiden. Tara, don't splash."

Two teenage girls in skimpy bikinis approached, their long, tan legs moving in stride. What he would give to be a young man in this day and age. But they paid him no attention, some stupid old man in long sleeve shirt and pants. A smile and a wave from him would turn their stomachs.

When his legs tired, he turned and headed back to the pier, its long silhouette stretching past the breaking waves. The old wooden one was destroyed by the hurricane, but the state stepped in and built a new one made of concrete.

He labored up the steps to find Melvin still behind the counter.

"Where's your better half?" Melvin asked.

"She passed."

"Oh, Lord. When did that happen?"

"Last month. She had a stroke."

Melvin shook his head. "Seems like a lot of the old crowd is passing on. Charley Mangum died. Did you know him?"

"Charley died?"

"He retired to his farm in Virginia. He was out with his backhoe, turned up a hornet's nest. They stung him to death before he could get back to the house."

He looked through the glass doors. "How do you like the new pier?"

"It's comfortable in here with the air conditioning. But concrete's not the same as wood. You can't feel the ocean no more."

He paid his dollar and walked outside. The pier was empty, except for a few fisherman scattered along the rail. The waves broke around the pilings as always, but Melvin was right. You couldn't feel a thing. He walked to the end. The ocean was calm all the way to the horizon, not a breath of wind. Waves rose from the depths as regular as a heartbeat, surged past the pillars and slid back again. The dizzy feeling he'd experienced on the footbridge came back, only this time he wasn't afraid. The truth was he didn't care if he lived or died. He wanted to be with Opal.

Sunday morning, he locked the trailer for the last time. He didn't bother to say goodbye to Harris. No point in upsetting him. He'd call Topsail Realty on Monday and ask them to list the trailer for whatever they thought it would bring. The new owner could fix it up or haul it to the dump.

* * *

When he pulled up to the house, he saw Renata in the front garden, a bale of straw and pile of newspaper at her side. He was expecting Danny. Renata hadn't ventured to his side of the drive since Opal died.

He put his suitcase inside and turned on the air conditioner, then walked out to the garden.

Renata smiled at his approach. "Are you back from the beach? You didn't stay very long."

"I was just checking on the trailer. Might need a new floor."

He pointed to the seed packets by her side. "What you got there?"

"Lima beans, snap beans. Marigold plants to keep the bugs away."

"You want some help with that newspaper?"

"Sure. If you don't mind."

He unfolded the papers and handed them to her. She laid them on the bare ground between the rows. "Danny not helping you?"

"Danny has moved out."

The blood rushed to his head. What had he done now?

"She's rented an apartment in town. In one of those converted tobacco warehouses." She held up her hands to make a quotation mark. " 'The New Durham.' "

"How long is she gonna stay?"

"I don't know. We'll see."

He untied a bale of straw and helped her spread that on top of the paper.

"I should be mad at you, but I guess I'm thankful," she said. "It would have been worse the longer it went on."

"Are you through with it?" he asked.

"I don't know. We'll see."

They worked on in silence.

"I'm selling the trailer at the beach," he said.

"Really? Why?"

"It ain't the same without Opal."

Renatta sighed. "I can see that."

She pointed across the road. "That public hearing on the rezoning is tomorrow night," she said. "Are you going to speak?"

"Nah."

"Gosh, I'd have thought you'd be against this thing. What's going on?"

He considered how much to reveal about his conversation with Linwood. Best to be truthful. "Developer says he'll hire Buddy's company to do the grading if the project goes through. I got to think about my boy. He's got a mortgage to pay."

"So they asked you not to say anything against it?"

"Manner of speaking."

She stared at him. "Wow. O.K."

"You say what you want at the hearing," he said. "I ain't gonna hold it against you."

Chapter 53

In his 70 years in Durham, Hurley had never stepped inside the courthouse. It made him nervous to come downtown with all the colored people. He wasn't sure who was here because of committing some crime or just doing official business.

He asked the policeman inside for the location of the hearing.

"Second floor. Take the elevator."

He packed in with a mixed bunch of colored and white. Some of them joked back and forth. They must work together.

The doors opened and he found himself swept along into the hearing room. There was a big crowd, some of whom he recognized. Linwood stood in the center aisle shaking hands. That man seemed to know everyone. Brady Grovenstein and his wife sat up front. They owned the property to the south of Marvin's. And there was Renata. He knew she was here to speak against the project, so he took a seat on the other side of the aisle. Just before the hearing started, Danny came in and stood in the back.

At the front of the room, thirteen council members sat behind a podium. Half of them were colored, one was a woman. Mayor MacAfee sat in the middle, blonde-haired, blue-eyed, flashing a big smile like the world was his oyster.

On an easel up front, the developer had put up a drawing of Marvin's lot. Hurley recognized the shape of it, but not much else. Roads curved every which way surrounded by dozens of houses. The sight of it made him sick, but he had to remember Linwood's promise.

MacAfee called the meeting to order. He explained what the hearing was for and asked for a report by the city planner. The planner talked about how Durham needed more housing for all the people that were moving in to work in the Research Triangle Park. He said the city's long-range plan called for "increasing density" in the southern part of town, and that the city would be running water and sewer lines all the way down Hope Valley Road.

He then introduced the developer from Charlotte, Wade something or other. The man got up rubbing his scalp like he had lice.

"I want to thank you all for inviting me here," Wade said. "I'm so proud to have the chance to do a project in Durham."

Hurley chuckled at that. The only thing that man was proud of was getting the land cheap. Wade went on to talk about Marvin's land and how it was ideal for a "mixed-use" development. He said he could cluster houses on certain parts of the property and leave the rest as "open space." By the looks of the drawing, the only open space was the bottom land along the creek, which Hurley knew to be covered in privet. Wasn't anything open about it.

The man boasted how he would leave a "vegetative buffer" around the edge of the property. Hurley didn't think there were any vegetables except in Marvin's old garden, and most of that had grown up in weeds. Still, he was glad the developer wasn't planning to build houses right up to the road.

Wade sat down and MacAfee called on interested citizens to come up to the podium and speak. First up was some lady with a fancy hairdo who said she lived on Hope Valley Road up near the country club. She said she already had trouble getting out of her driveway on weekday mornings and that all the traffic from a new development would only make matters worse. He didn't doubt that, but seeing as he never went out before noon, he figured he could live with it. Next up was some Duke professor in a blue blazer and yellow tie. He said he could understand the need for more housing, but thought that the rezoning needed more study. A fellow with long hair worried that the development would increase run-off into New Hope Creek. Hurley couldn't figure out why that would bother anyone. It wasn't anything but a muddy old creek to begin with.

Finally, Renata came forward. She took a deep breath and in a quavering voice, began to speak. "My name is Renata Torres and I live across the street from the lot you see here. I work in Research Triangle Park, in a lab with no windows, so I never see the sun. When I wake up in the morning, one of my great pleasures is to look out across the valley and see Marvin's pasture. Some mornings, there's a mist hanging over it. When I come home in the afternoon, I see the shadows of the trees across the grass. I know most of you can't share that view from your homes, but I believe that everyone who drives down Hope Valley Road gains something by seeing this land in its natural state. Maybe it can't stay exactly as it is. Maybe it could be broken into five-acre lots or something like that. But the thought of covering it all with houses just breaks my heart." He felt a lump rise in his throat. "So often, it seems, we don't miss the beauty in our lives until it's gone. And once it's gone, once this land is gone, it's never coming back. So I'm asking you, my friends and neighbors, and you the commissioners, to have the courage and foresight to preserve what is beautiful. Don't rezone this land."

Renata thanked the council and went back to her seat. MacAfee asked if anyone else wanted to speak. Hurley looked around the room. Danny had left. Was no one going to speak in favor of the rezoning?

"Do I hear a motion to close the hearing?"

The council members raised their hands. The hearing was closed.

As the audience filed out of the room, he found Linwood in a corner.

"How come nobody spoke in favor?" he said. "If I'd a known, I might have said something."

Linwood seemed unconcerned. "That's the way these hearings go. Only the people who are opposed to a change speak out."

He put a hand on Hurley's shoulder. "Don't you worry," he said. "A little birdie told me everything's going to be al-l-right."

Chapter 54

Two months after the hearing, the council approved the rezoning. The developer broke ground the following week, the chainsaws starting just after dawn. He looked out the bedroom window to see a herd of deer sprint across the road and up his yard. They'd struggle to survive in the woods behind his house, raiding the vegetable garden every chance they got.

Buddy said he'd be taking down Marvin's house first thing. This would be the first time Hurley'd ever had the chance to visit his son on a job site and it was something he didn't want to miss.

As he stepped out onto the porch, he saw the tractor trailer with the track hoe pull into the drive. He headed down the hill with Gus trailing behind.

"Go on back to the house!" he said.

The old dog limped away.

Traffic was thick on Hope Valley since they'd opened the freeway interchange. He waited for a break in the line of cars, then hurried across.

Down by the house, Buddy leaned against the trailer talking with the truck driver.

"This here's my Pa," Buddy said by way of introduction. "He used to be a friend of Marvin's."

The truck driver offered his hand. "Sorry to hear about your friend." He shook his head. "This must be the fifth farmhouse we've taken down this year. Seems like a generation is passing."

"You want anything out of the house?" Buddy asked.

"What do I want of Marvin's?"

"There's some bathroom fixtures."

He scoffed. "I don't need but one place to shit."

Buddy climbed into the cab of the track hoe and fired up the diesel engine. While the truck driver waved him on, he backed the machine off the trailer, spun it 90 degrees, and rumbled toward the house.

He sat for a moment studying the structure, then he pulled on a lever. The arm rose and the jaws opened. Hurley winced as the teeth punched through the roof of the house. Plywood shattered. Rafters snapped. The jaws pulled the roof to the ground and the inside of Marvin's home was revealed.

Buddy tore open the living room with its the green patterned wallpaper and then the bedroom, its south wall spattered with Marvin's blood. Another thing a man wasn't supposed to see.

When he looked again, the house lay in a heap. Only the brick chimney remained. Ever so gently, Buddy pivoted the arm against the chimney and, with a tweak of a lever, knocked it over.

"That's the end of that," the driver said.

Buddy set about separating out the metal appliances and porcelain fixtures—things that wouldn't burn. In one fluid motion, he picked up the toilet, set it upright to one side, then went back for the sink and the tub. Hurley marveled how under Buddy's control, the claw seemed not some separate piece of machinery, but an extension of Buddy's hand.

"He's pretty good with that, ain't he?" he said.

The driver nodded. "About the best."

"Is that right?"

"In this area, I'd say so. I ain't seen anyone can handle a track hoe like Buddy Cates."

Without warning, his eyes brimmed with tears. Nobody had ever said anything like that about Buddy.

Chapter 55

"Mom! Mom!" Noah's voice rang out as he ran across the lawn to greet Danny. She opened her arms, drew her son close, and felt his heartbeat against her chest. Then Noah disappeared around a corner, the yard breaking into fragments. Danny opened her eyes and remembered once again that her son was dead.

And that she was alone. She stared at the apartment's high ceilings, exposed ductwork, brick wall, and the single metal-mullioned window. The developers had done a decent job converting this tobacco warehouse to apartments. She ought to get some rugs, some furniture beside the mattress and the dinette set. But she rather liked idea of leading the ascetic life—Saint Jerome in his cave, translating the Bible.

She rolled off the mattress onto the shellacked heartpine floor and pulled himself to her feet. From outside the door, she retrieved the newspaper and tossed it on the dinette table. *Two Dead in Walltown Shootout.* Good old Durham. One step forward, two steps back. At least the shootings took place on the other side of town.

She wondered what Hurley would think of this apartment complex. It would probably just make him sad. In his day, American Tobacco was one big space full of humming machinery and people. The jobs might have been tedious, but the workers formed bonds. Now, it was all sectioned off, full of people like her living in isolation.

She opened the refrigerator, bare except for a pint of orange juice and a carton of milk. She sniffed at the milk. Oof! She ought to get herself a new carton, but that would mean getting dressed, going out to the car, and driving a mile to Sam's Convenience Store. This was another challenge of being a pioneer in downtown Durham—no grocery stores.

She poured herself some Cheerios and stomached the sour milk. It might make her sick, but it wouldn't kill her—a sufficient goal these days.

Against the wall by the front door stood a pile of manuscripts gleaned from the Divinity School Library. Danny had not published in more than a year. To maintain her standing in the field, she needed to produce something and all she had at this point was a title: *Preterism, Pre-millenialism, and Other Variations on The Notion of End Times.* Oh, yes, very important. Based on scripture, many Christians and Jews believed there would come a time of social collapse, of corruption and sin—the end days—predating the return of the Messiah. But others, the Preterists for one, suggest this is a misreading of scripture, that the term really is not "end time" but rather "a time of the end" referring to the end of the covenant between God and Israel, not the end of human life. The time of the end is already past, AD70 to be exact, when the Jewish Temple was destroyed. But there are Preterists and Partial Preterists, Millenialists and Pre-Millenialists. Thus, the stack of books. Thus, her massive headache.

Danny grabbed the first book and began wading through it, taking notes with pen and paper. Around noon, she heard the door open in the apartment next door. Through the wall came the muffled greeting of his neighbor, a professor of Anthropology. "Come in! Make yourself at home!" Noise was a problem with these apartments. The developers had lavished money on many features, but they'd skimped on the common walls. And the open ductwork functioned like a megaphone.

A burst of girlish laughter led to a teasing basso response. Great. The prof had lured another kitten to his lair. He'd done this half-a-dozen times in the past month and it was always a noisy affair. Danny guessed these women were students. She knew the dynamics all too well.

Another round of laughter gave way to a prolonged silence and what she imagined as "the kiss." The memory of Renata's infidelity came rushing back. Maybe this prof didn't have a wife, but this student, this girl, would be damaged goods from here on out. Any compliment the teacher might give her, any grade, would be poisoned by the notion that he was just doing it to get laid.

Then, the groaning started. It came from the overhead vent which, she imagined, was connected by the heating duct to a similar vent over her neighbor's bed. It started out with soft panting and rose to a shuddering, animalistic moan. On and on this guy went. What was he, Superman? Danny slammed her book closed. She slid her chair under the vent, stood on the seat and yelled. "People are trying to work here!"

The moaning stopped. She tried to get back to work, but it was no good. She had to get away. She grabbed her sunglasses and hat and stormed out of the apartment into the heat of a July afternoon.

Along Hope Valley Road with its archway of oaks, the air temperature began to drop. The brick mansions with their circular drives seemed to exude a sense of calm. Just beyond the city limits, the mansions gave way to bungalows and finally, to the farmhouse and the ranch house side by side at the top of the hill.

As she pulled up the drive, she noted the weeds springing up in the yard. Hurley would be upset about that. She parked in front of the car shed and stepped out into the heat. Renata was gone to work, Hurley probably napping. The buzz of cicadas filled the humid air.

Gus emerged from under his bush, so stiff-legged he could barely walk. She knelt down and kissed his graying muzzle.

"You miss me, don't you, boy?"

The riding lawn mower sat in the back of the shed, its seat covered in dust. She wiped it off with her shirt sleeve, sat down and turned the key. Nothing. She wheeled the mower into the sunlight and lifted the cowl. A blue-green powder caked the battery posts. She retrieved the toolbox from the back of the car, unscrewed the battery wires, and filed the posts clean. She removed the air filter and banged it against the side of the shed. This time, the engine started right up. She set the mower in third, rumbled between the two houses, and onto the lawn.

For most of the time she'd lived here, she'd considered mowing the lawn a chore. There was always something else she'd rather be doing. But now, she relaxed behind the wheel, content to devote herself to this simple task. She rode slowly downhill, the hum of the engine resonating through her body. The grass and weeds passed beneath her, emerging as a uniform carpet of green. She reached the road and turned, rumbled back to the top and turned again. Like the sunlight through the canopy of the oaks, her thoughts scattered and soon, she had none.

Chapter 56

By late October, the landscaping for Marvin's Run was all but finished. The roads were laid out. Builders had started framing houses. Hurley was sitting on his porch listening to the thwack of hammers when Linwood turned in the drive.

The realtor was all smiles, his wallet no doubt stuffed with cash.

"How ya' doing, Hurley? Just thought I'd pay you a visit."

He motioned Linwood to sit.

"They sure are moving fast over there," Linwood said. "Houses are already going up."

"Sold any yet?"

Linwood smiled. "Sold a few."

He stuffed a chaw in his cheek. "'Preciate what you did for Buddy."

"He's doing a fine job over there. Be finished in another week. Ready for the next job."

A breeze sent a scattering of crimson leaves from the wood's edge onto the lawn.

"Did you hear you're going to be incorporated into the city?" Linwood said.

"I read about it."

Linwood shook his head. "There go the taxes. Do you know that Durham's got the highest property tax rate in the state?"

"Politicians gotta pay off their voters."

"I also heard we're due for a revaluation."

"Hell you say."

"Oh yeah. This time they're going to use current value. Now that you got water and sewer and development across the way, this'll be considered prime development property. Your taxes could more than double."

Linwood bounced his hands between his knees. "Of course, that works both ways. If you were to sell your property, you'd walk away with a pile of money. I have it on good word that Wade would be interested in buying this place. Your neighbor's, too."

He glared. "What am I gonna do with a pile of money? I got what I need right here."

Linwood shook his head. "Last again," he said.

"How's that?"

"You're the last farm on Hope Valley Road."

He spat. Linwood rose.

"I just thought I'd pass on that information. Are your neighbors home?"

"Renata might be around. Danny don't stay here no more."

"Oh, really?"

* * *

When Hurley went out to get the paper, Renata was standing in the drive petting Gus' head. The dog stood in a spread-eagled stance, his eyes blurry. As Hurley approached, the dog started to cough.

"Something's wrong with Gus," she said. "He's gagging but nothing's coming out."

He frowned. "He didn't eat last night. His stomach looks swole up. Maybe he got into a dead squirrel."

Renata put her hand under his stomach. "God, it's tight as a drum. No wonder he's in pain."

"I'm going down to get the paper. After breakfast, I'll carry him on over to the vet."

"You don't want to take him now?"

"Nah."

Shannon Road Veterinary was busy on a Saturday morning, old women cradling small dogs, a girl with a cat in a cage. He checked in at the desk and sat next to a woman with a fat Beagle. Gus cowered between his feet as the beagle strained at his leash.

"You be nice, Beasley."

A woman came through the front door and approached the desk attendant in a hushed voice. "I'm here for Shelley," she said.

The attendant took down a blue urn from a shelf behind the counter and handed it to the woman. "I'm so sorry," she said.

"Gus?" The vet stood in the hallway with a clipboard.

"That's me," Hurley said.

He followed the vet down the hall and into the tiny examination room. The vet closed the door. "What seems to be the problem?"

"Belly's swole up. He don't want to eat."

The vet kneeled down and spoke to Gus, rubbing him between the ears. "You're a good dog, aren't you? You just don't understand what's going on."

He rolled Gus onto his back and felt his stomach. "How old is this dog?"

"Probably twelve or thirteen. I don't recollect."

"Do you know how long his stomach's been like this?"

"Might be just today. My neighbor noticed it this morning."

"I'm afraid the news isn't good," the vet said. "He's got bloat. His stomach has actually twisted over and it's cutting off the entry or exit of anything into or out of the stomach. He will actually die in short order if we don't do surgery. And I have to tell you the surgery is quite expensive."

"How much?"

"More than a thousand dollars."

He shook his head. "Dog ain't worth that kind of money."

"That's why I asked about his age. You can leave him here with us and we'll take care of him this evening."

Gus looked at him with fear in his eyes. Hurley looked away.

"There's no charge for euthanasia," the vet said, "But if you want him cremated and the ashes returned, there is a charge."

"I don't need no ashes."

"Alright, then. Would you like a minute alone with Gus."

He shook his head. "He's just a farm dog. I start rubbing his head he'll know something's up."

With that, he stood and shook the vet's hand. "You stay here," he said to Gus, trying to maintain his usual gruff tone. "Let the man take care of you."

* * *

Hurley's head spun as he drove down the road. He knew he'd done the right thing. Still, Gus's last look haunted him. The dog knew what was happening. He knew Hurley was leaving him to die.

Instead of driving home, he turned into Taylor's Exxon. He needed to talk.

Russell was changing a tire, so he took a seat in the office. He fished a Coke out of the cooler and stuck his head through the door to the service bay.

"You mind?" he said, holding the drink up.

"Help yourself," Russell said. "I'll be there in a minute."

Russell came in and wrote up a ticket. "What's going on, Hurley?"

"I just dropped Gus off to get put down. He's got the stomach bloat."

Russell finished with the ticket and dropped it in a basket. "I'm sorry to hear that."

"Vet said they only thing they could do was surgery and that'd cost over a thousand dollars."

Russell whistled. "That's a lot of money to spend on a dog."

"What I told him. They're gonna put him down this afternoon."

"You're really gonna be alone on that hill now," Russell said.

He sipped on his Coke and looked out the window. "Jernigan stopped by the other day. Trying to get me to sell the farm. Said that developer over at Marvin's give me a good price for it."

Russell raised an eyebrow. "What'd you say to that?"

"Where am I gonna go if I sell the farm?"

"You could find somewhere further out in the county. Get away from all this development."

He shook his head. "Something'll come after you wherever you go."

He finished his Coke and set it in the rack.

"You ever think of moving to a retirement home?" Russell asked.

"Might as well put a bullet in my head like old Marvin."

"You'd be popular with the ladies."

"Pshaw."

"I'm serious. I hear a healthy man in a retirement home is like a beefsteak to a pack of hounds."

"If my dick could get as stiff as my back I might be interested, but I ain't."

Russell laughed. "You may be right."

Danny's car was in the drive when he arrived. Both he and Renata were raking leaves in the back yard. This was the first time he'd seen them together since Danny left in May.

Danny greeted him as he stepped out of the truck. "What's the story with Gus?"

"Stomach's all twisted up. Vet said it's best to put him down."

Renata stared. "You left him?"

"That's right."

"What about surgery?" Danny said. "Can't they do anything?"

"For a thousand dollars? I ain't gonna spend that kind of money on an old dog."

The women exchanged glances.

"I'll pay for it, if that's the issue," Danny said.

"He's an old dog. Can't hardly shit. I ain't interested in nursing him."

"What if we took him?" Renata said. "Made him our responsibility?"

He shrugged. "You can try. Might be too late."

"What's the name of the vet?" Danny said.

Chapter 57

The women saved Gus. They paid for the surgery and brought him home the next day. Renata confronted Hurley in the driveway. "I'm going to take over the feeding. And I'm going to let him stay inside at night, if that's O.K. with you."

"I don't ever let a dog inside, but you do what you want."

The day before, Renata had said she was going to make Gus "our" responsibility. Something had changed between her and Danny. He hadn't seen the man since Danny left, so at least he was out of the picture.

"Linwood talk to you the other day?" he asked.

"Yes. He wants to buy our land. I told him we weren't interested."

"What about you?" she asked. "Are you thinking of selling?"

"I might. It's a lot to take care of. Taxes are supposed to go way up."

She watched him for a moment, her face growing dark.

"There's something I haven't told you," she said. "We scattered Noah's ashes in the back field."

He looked up. "I thought you buried him."

"No. We had him cremated. We love it so much back there. It just seemed like the right place for him to be."

He gazed at the tractor path disappearing into the woods. Little Noah back there, scattered amongst the broomsage and rye.

* * *

The following week, he got the letter from the county notifying him of the property revaluation. His twenty acres were revalued at $400,000, up from $100,000. He called the assessor's office in a rage, demanded to know why it had gone up so much. The man said he was now in the city's low-density residential zoning district, which computed the land at $20,000 an acre. He insisted his was nothing but a farm. The man said to qualify for an agricultural zoning, he would have to be able to show revenue of at least $1,000 a year from the sale of farm products. Unless somebody was willing to pay for lawn clippings, he could not come close to that.

"What's my tax gonna be?"

The man took a minute to make his calculations. "Your city tax will be $6,000 a year, and there'll be a county tax on top of that."

"I ain't got that kind of money."

"Sir, if you would like to file an official complaint, you will need to send a letter to the tax assessors office."

A few days later, he got a letter welcoming him to the City of Durham, signed by Mayor Wib MacAfee. He balled it up and threw it in the wastebasket. A minute later, he retrieved it, thinking it might somehow be helpful if he had some problem with the city in the future.

There was another letter, this one from Wade Properties. He opened it slowly and flattened it on the kitchen table. The man was offering to purchase his property for $500,000. He read the number three times to make sure he hadn't miscounted the zeros. On the margin, Wade had written in pen, "Very pleased with Buddy's work on Marvin's Run. Will certainly consider using him again."

* * *

Hurley stepped out the porch on a gray November day and stared across the valley. A whooshing noise filled the air. He glanced at the tops of the pines, bending to a wind he couldn't feel. Used to be the change of seasons got his energy up, but not anymore. Nothing lasted. The lawn, the buildings, the trees—all those things he'd nurtured for so many years would soon be gone, whether by his hand or someone else's.

He stepped off the porch and wandered back past the neighbor's house. Gus hobbled out to greet him. Together they walked out the tractor path to the back field.

Beneath the overcast sky, the field took on pale shades of yellow and brown. Brambles were starting to take hold. The gardens were overgrown. Was this where they'd scattered the ashes? He walked among the weeds and grasses, his ankles bending atop the hummocks.

He turned and startled. Renata stood behind him. "You scared me, girl."

"I followed you out."

She waited with her hands in the pockets of her dark pea jacket.

"I come to see where you put Noah's ashes."

"We spread them on the garden." She studied the rows beneath the crabgrass. "Somehow I imagined that if I planted the garden again and ate the new seeds that I would have a part of Noah inside me."

He nodded. "You got a whole lot of Noah inside you."

She smiled. He felt a rush of warmth. Maybe she'd forgiven him.

"I got a letter from Wade," he said.

She nodded. "We got one, too."

"What's he offering you?"

"$200,000."

He shook his head. "That's a lot of money. What are you planning to do?"

"That depends on what you do, I guess," she said. "I wouldn't want to stay here if your property is developed."

"What's Danny want to do?"

"I don't know. I told her about the letter. She said she needed to think about it."

"You ain't apologized?"

She looked at the ground. "Apologies aren't always enough."

The warmth he'd sensed in her before seemed to be gone.

"I think we need to have a meeting to talk about this," she said. "All three of us."

"A meeting?"

"Yes. Soon."

Chapter 58

All day long, Hurley fretted about how to respond to Wade's offer. Desperate for any kind of distraction, he decided to sharpen the mower blades. He put on his jacket and stepped outside. A cold front was coming in, a breeze rattling the leaves on the beech trees at the edge of the woods. Gus appeared, a faint wag in his tail. He rubbed the dog's head. "You ain't gonna give up yet, are you boy?"

On the way out to the barn, a squirrel scampered across the drive. Gus followed the scent to the base of the tree, never breaking into a run. Old dogs were like old people. They still had a taste for the hunt, but weren't up to the chase.

He dug the ramps out of the back of the barn and set them near the door where the light was good. He drove the John Deere onto the ramps, grabbed a crescent wrench and lay on his back in the dirt. The first nut came off easy. The second refused to budge. He wedged a block of wood between the blade and housing and gave the wrench a hard twist. Nothing. He pulled as hard as he could. The wrench slipped, his knuckles raking across the blade.

"God...dang!"

He rolled out from under the mower and examined his fingers. Blood pooled atop the knuckles. He'd need to bandage those up. And he ought not try to remove those blades. Let Taylor's do that with a power wrench.

When Hurley arrived, Russell was in the service bay underneath a car. He expressed disbelief that Hurley was actually going to pay for something besides a tank of gas.

"That nut must be real tight," he said.

Hurley got a Coke from the office and sat in a chair besides the tool chest.

"I got a letter from Wade," he said. "Guess what he's offering?"

"I don't know. $300,000?"

"Way off."

"400,000."

"You're getting' warmer."

Russell slid out from under the car. "He's offering more than $400,000?"

Hurley grinned. "$500,000."

"Holy shit. You're going to take it, right?"

"I don't know."

"Man, you could get yourself a nice condo in Dunbarton Oaks and a club membership to boot."

"My neighbors got a letter, too. I'm supposed to meet with them tonight. We're gonna talk it out."

"Talk it out? Are you depending on them to tell you what to do?"

He sniffed. "I can make up my own mind."

A man wearing a tweed jacket and leather gloves appeared in the doorway. He gave Hurley a furtive glance. "Is Russell here?"

"He's under the car."

Russell slid out and wiped off his hands. "Mr. Price. What can I do for you?"

"I'd like to have my tires rotated. What's your schedule?"

"I could do it tomorrow."

"I'll be by in the morning."

The man gave him another look, then headed out the door.

"Is he Duke?" Hurley asked.

"Yup. A professor."

"You can always tell Duke. They've got their noses in the air."

"He actually puts some money in the register."

Russell slid out from under the car. "Speaking of Duke, are you going to watch the game tonight?"

"I might. We get through with this meeting."

"Duke's pretty good this year. I like that Christian Laettner."

"He's alright."

"I'd sure like to get to one of those games."

"Pshaw. You won't see the inside of Cameron unless you write a thousand dollar check to the Iron Dukes. Get you a seat in the back row."

"That may be right."

"You know I'm right."

He savored his small moment of certainty. The big decision still loomed. He stood to go.

"I'll leave that mower in back," he said. "Call me when it's ready."

Chapter 59

Danny knocked on the door of the house on Sparger Road. Leanne answered in curlers.

"Hello, there," Leanne said. "Nice to see you on this side of town."

They shook hands.

"Buddy's in the kitchen. I've got to head out and do some shopping."

She walked into the sunlit kitchen and found Buddy sitting at the table with his Bible. He offered her some juice. She took off her winter coat and hung it on the back of the chair.

"How are you liking this cool weather?" Buddy asked.

"It's alright. My place is a little chilly with those high ceilings."

"Where's that you're staying?"

"South Village."

They talked about all the building renovations going on downtown. Hearing Leanne go out the door, she changed the subject.

"Listen, I feel really bad about the way we left things in September. You and Dwayne came over to express your condolences and we never offered our thanks."

Buddy pulled on his ear. "Renata seemed pretty angry."

"She blames everyone, including herself."

"I should have told those boys to play next door. A man ought to know better than to let young 'uns on a work site."

"Believe me, not a day goes by when I haven't second guessed myself. It'll eat you alive if you let it. It's eating Renata."

Buddy shook his head. "I wish there was something I could do."

They sat together, hands on their foreheads. "You lost someone, too," she said. "Your sister, Patsy."

Buddy looked up, surprised. "That was awhile back."

"What was the story with her? I got some hints that she was like me."

He nodded. "She was what we called a tomboy. Never did like playing with dolls or any of that. Never had a boyfriend. I guess she was a lesbian."

"Did she ever come out?"

"She said something to Ma and Pa after she was out of school. They would never tell me exactly what, but they pretty much shunned her after that. She moved to Raleigh and lived by herself. She had a job for awhile with the state. I thought she was alright. Then we heard she committed suicide."

She shook her head. "Did your parents talk to anyone about her? Get some advice?"

"They talked to the preacher at some point. He said it was a sin and that they ought to try to get her to change."

She snorted. "Typical."

"I don't think they ever accepted who she was. I'm sure that was a big part of why she committed suicide. They never owned up to that either, but they must have known."

"Do you think that's why your Dad was so overly protective of you?"

"Could be. I got picked on a lot when I was young. Me and Patsy were both different."

She looked out the window at the bare trees, thought of how Patsy's death and Buddy's departure lead to her acceptance by the Cates. "Your parents sure changed," she said. "They were cool to us at first, but they really warmed up, especially your Dad."

He nodded. "Pa's a good man."

"Listen, you asked if there was anything you could do..."

Chapter 60

It was coming on dark by the time Danny's car pulled up. He waited a few minutes, then grabbed his letter and crossed the drive. The smell of wood smoke let him know there was a fire inside. Renata answered the door and invited him in.

The first thing he noticed was the photo of Noah on the wall. He was seated on the tire swing, grinning at the camera.

Danny sat on the couch. "Can we get you something to drink?" she asked.

"Water'd be fine."

She reached into a brown paper bag and pulled out a bottle of Jack Daniel's. "How about some of this to go with it?"

He shook his head. "I ain't supposed to drink."

"Says who?"

He grinned. "Alright. Just a tad."

She got up and went to the kitchen, where Renata was laying out cheese and crackers. "You like it with ice?"

"Oh, yeah."

He took off his coat and sat on the couch holding his letter. Danny handed him the glass, the whiskey glowing in the warm firelight. He took a sip, felt the delicious burn in his stomach.

"That's alright," he said.

Renata poured herself a glass of wine and set the cheese and crackers on the table. She took a chair at the dining table.

"So how do we want to go about this?" she said.

Danny reached out. "Do you mind if I read your letter?"

He pushed it forward. "Go ahead."

She read it, whistling at the end. "Wow. $500,000. That is an insane amount of money. Oh, and here's a little bribe to go with it. 'Very pleased with Buddy's work. Look forward to using him in the future.' "

She set the letter down on the table. "Hard to say no to that."

"I don't need the money," he said. "But I've got to look out for my boy."

Renata looked dejected. She poured herself a second glass of wine. Danny raised the Jack to Hurley.

"Another one for you?"

He held up his glass.

"What if I told you that Buddy doesn't need this extra work?" Danny said.

"What are you talking about?"

"I went to see Buddy yesterday. We talked about Wade's offer. He's deeply moved that you would consider selling the farm just to help him out. But he told me with all the new construction going on at Duke, he's going to be busy for the next year."

"You talk him into this?"

She shook her head. "I said I could live with it either way."

He pondered the situation. "I've still got those taxes to think about. Man at the city said I'll be paying close to $6,000 a year."

"I've been doing some thinking about that," Danny said. "Durham has a provision where if you can show at least a thousand dollars a year in sale of agricultural products, you qualify as a farm for tax purposes."

"What am I gonna do, set up a stand down by the road sell tomatoes?"

"No. Plant a corn maze."

"A corn maze?"

"In the back field. I've been reading up on these things. People can make a bunch of money on these. You plant the corn in the early summer and it's ready by July. You can bring in church groups, school kids..."

"Excuse me?" Renata said. "What are you talking about?"

Danny went on. "We only open the maze in the fall for about a month. It wouldn't be that much work."

"What do you mean by 'we'?" Renata said.

Danny stopped, glanced at him. "Maybe Renata and I ought to have this conversation in private."

He nodded. "I can come back another time."

"No, let's have it now." Renata was half-drunk, waving her glass of wine in the air. "You can't just come in here and propose things like this and expect people to agree."

Danny sighed. She bounced her hands up and down, looked Renata in the eye. "I want to come back. I want to try and be a family again. All of us."

Renata teared up. "Really? You forgive me?" She came off the chair and wrapped her arms around Danny.

Hurley's head spun. There was something *he* wanted to say. He took another drink. "I'm sorry I killed your boy. I should've hired that job out."

Renata sagged onto the floor. She turned her hands up. "And I should've been watching him, but I went inside."

Danny shook her head. "We all fucked up."

"I killed my daughter, too," he said. "I turned her away when she needed me."

He closed his eyes, tears streaming down his cheeks. He couldn't stand the thought of what she might have become if she'd lived long enough. He felt a strong hand on his shoulder, then a softer pair on the back of his neck. Renata pressed her cheek to his.

"I love you, Hurley."

Chapter 61

Russell looked up from his paper. "A corn maze?"

"That's right," Hurley said. "We plant nine acres of that, another acre of pumpkins. That'll give us ten for the agricultural zoning."

"How much do you think you'll make?"

"Three or four thousand on the maze, another thousand on the pumpkins."

"Who's going to plant all that?"

"Buddy'll put in the maze. He's got a friend with a planter. Me and Renata will put in the pumpkins."

"She's going to quit her job to manage all this?"

"We'll trade off at the cash box. I'm gonna put up a pole barn out there to keep us out of the sun."

He finished his Coke and dropped the bottle in the garbage.

"We recycle those now," Russell said. "Put it in that crate."

He fished the bottle out. "Got me a ticket to the game tonight."

"The Duke game?"

"Danny got three tickets. Early season. East Carolina."

In the afternoon, he walked to the back field to see how the scheme might play out. There would be a parking area to the right and the pole building to the left. The field, nine acres of it anyway, would be corn. Danny had found a book of designs, so you could plant a different maze every year. He imagined the children racing in between the green stalks. Some of them would come back discouraged, small shoulders slumped.

"Keep on trying," he'd say. "It ain't meant to be easy."

* * *

Cameron Indoor Stadium was packed. He followed Danny and Renata through the narrow hall, wearing the Blue Devil cap Danny had given him back at the house. He stared at the faces coming the other way. There was the manager from Nations Bank. And Linwood. He reached out and stopped him.

"How'ya doing, Linwood."

Linwood put on a smile. "Fine, fine. Hope you are, too. Got to get to my seat."

Danny led the way to the concession stand, where she bought him a Coke for $2, then led the way through the portal. Cameron was louder than he'd imagined, hot and close. He sat next to Renata, the smell of patchouli rising as she shed her coat. She was all dressed up for the game, black stockings and black leather boots.

Across the way, a sea of blue painted faces hollered and sang. The pep band pounded out a tune. Cheerleaders dressed in miniskirts waved their pom-poms. Down on the court, the Blue Devils ran through their warm-ups. There was Christian Laettner, as tall and handsome as he looked on TV, a shock of brown hair falling across his brow. Grant Hill strolled in for a lay up, smooth as butter. At the top of the key, Bobby Hurley lobbed in baskets with mechanical precision.

The announcer called for people to stand as the national anthem played on the PA. When the song came to the line about the star-spangled banner, all the students shouted, "Oh!" in unison. He was shocked at the disrespect, but Renata touched him on the arm.

"They always say that," she said.

As the anthem came to a close, a cheer went up and a loud thumping swelled through the stands. Coach K sent the starting team into the court. The referee tossed up the ball and the game was underway.

The score went back and forth for the first half, Duke missing some easy shots. Coach K got off the bench and snarled at his players.

"He kinda does look like a rat," he said to Renata.

At half time, the cheerleaders ran to the near side of the court. They wore tight tops and short skirts. He liked the second one in line, a kind of Chinese-looking gal. You didn't see many of them around.

The second half turned into a rout with Duke scoring every other possession. Bobby Hurley shredded the Pirates' defense. Laettner hit his outside jumper. Grant Hill took an alley-oop pass and slammed the ball through the net. Hurley jumped to his feet. "That's what I'm talkin' 'bout!"

After the game, as they walked toward the car, Danny put his arm around his shoulder. "What did you think, man?"

"That was alright."

"You're a Blue Devil now."

He climbed in the back seat of the Subaru, his knees pulled up to his chest. He stared at the silhouette of the pines on Hope

Valley Road. Opal would have been tickled to know he finally went to a Duke game. He missed that more than anything, coming into the kitchen, Opal's pretty face, expectant, wanting to hear what he'd seen.

In the driveway, he bid Danny and Renata goodnight. They let Gus out, the old dog hobbling into the frozen yard to pee. The night was clear and cold, headed down into the teens. He grabbed a couple of pieces wood from the stack by the car shed and went inside.

Kneeling before the woodstove, he realized he was still wearing Danny's Blue Devil cap. He went back across the drive, eager to recite a line he'd just thought up—"I ain't a Devil all the time!"

Gus stood by the door, waiting to be let back in. He was about to knock when through the window, he saw Renata and Danny in the middle of the room, engaged in an open-mouthed kiss.

Gus stared up at him, waiting for the door to open. Hurley leaned over and picked him up.

"Let's go back to the house," he said. "Leave them women be."

Acknowledgements

Many people have offered input toward this book in the decade it took to write. I would especially like to thank Anna Jean Mayhew for her final editing and Cathy Murphy for her proofreading. Thanks also to Laurel Goldman who, along with members of her writing class, including Betty Palmerton, A.J. Mayhew, Mia Bray, Fabienne Worth, Eve Rizzo, Cindy Paris, and Cat Warren, critiqued this manuscript in its early stages. Thanks also to Matthew Keuter, Thomas Jones, Edward Morrison, and Helen Bryce for their excellent editorial comments.

Photo by Cathy Murphy

About the Author

John Manuel grew up in Gates Mills, Ohio, and graduated from Yale University and the University of North Carolina at Chapel Hill. He now lives in Durham, NC, with his wife, Cathy. John has been a freelance writer since 1990, the majority of his journalistic stories being published in *Environmental Health Perspectives*, *Canoe&Kayak* and *Wildlife in North Carolina*. His short stories and creative non-fiction have appeared in the Savannah Anthology and the New Southerner. John is the author of two non-fiction books: *The Natural Traveler Along North Carolina's Coast* and *The Canoeist: A Memoir*.

CPSIA information can be obtained
at www.ICGtesting.com
Printed in the USA
LVOW12s1806151216
517423LV00005B/999/P